THE DEPTHS
OF
MY DELUSION

BY

KHALIL KALIFA

COPYRIGHT

DEDICATIONS

This book is dedicated to all the victims of slavery, war, and genocide, especially the Shoah and Nakba, their casualties and survivors, and all of their descendants.

This work acknowledges the associations between empire and slavery, progress and victimhood, colonization and mass murder, civilization and the nature of organic life.

For native America and the great gap in world culture when history was changed and we lost touch with their knowledge, respect for Earth and her many important creatures, and their wise and beautiful spirits.

For all the victims of nuclear weapons and their poisonous effects. I hope that we all have learned from your suffering and honor your memory by ensuring that those cruel and brutal actions are never repeated.

For all the refugees and victims of forced displacement, state corruption or collapse, and the chaos of power preservation or systemic change.

For the doctors and medical professionals, volunteers and journalists, who venture into the chaos of warzones, and are only motivated by the most altruistic of intentions.

For the individuals and organizations that strive to restore order and justice in a world of biased politics, a blind economy, systemic racism, and unchecked greed.

To all of the people who suffered loss or injury, hunger or disease, isolation or loneliness, fear and trauma, suffering, struggle, or death in vain, God is with you and has not forgotten.

For the Earth and all of her native lifeforms.

And for all of those who came before, and for all who will come after – we are all together, somewhere in time.

For God, and all of his knowledge, layers, and aspects. We hope and strive to be more like you - immortal, aware, perfectly balanced, content in our existence, and true to your designs and intentions.

ACKNOWLEDGEMENTS

Prophet Isaac

Moses

Zarathustra

Prophet Daniel

Jesus Christ

Muhammad ibn Abdullah (saw)

Saint Joan of Arc (Jeanne d'Arc)

Michel de Nostredame

And all of their predecessors, successors, companions, apostles, followers,

believers, scribes, co-authors, and audience.

Galileo Galilei

Isaac Newton

Albert Einstein

Neils Bohr

Stephen Hawking

Roger Penrose

Noam Chomsky

Norman Finkelstein

Jeffrey Sachs

Chris Hedges

Richard Wolff

Michael Hudson

John Mearsheimer

Roy Casagranda

Ray McGovern

John Perkins

Michael Moore

Karl Marx

John F. Kennedy

Bob Marley

Martin Luther King

Nelson Mandela

John Hogue

JRR Tolkien

Frank Herbert

Chuck Palahniuk

Lana (Larry) Wachowski

Lily (Andy) Wachowski

The Assassin's Creed franchise (Ubisoft)

TABLE OF CONTENTS

INTRODUCTION

I was born and raised in Ireland and began to experience constant and prominent auditory hallucinations from the age of eighteen. At the time I could not comprehend or process the experience at all. I had no understanding whatsoever of psychological disorder, and it seemed so convincing, and so real, that I just tolerated it. In a way, I had so many unusual experiences with people and friends growing up that it may not have seemed so implausible that I was being watched, or lied to and used, or deliberately distracted.

After twelve years, they had completely faded away, but an anomalous experience forced me to re-examine my entire life, and I could only arrive at the conclusion that I was the reincarnation of Jesus Christ. The more I analyzed my ordeals, and the reasons why I began hearing voices, the more plausible and logical that belief became. I started to understand his story through the lens of my own experiences, and felt that I got a glimpse of the forces that he was faced with, the reasons why he was killed, and even the rationale behind why he chose to face it, instead of just running away.

We are all learning about religion, prophets, Messianic figures, and God from a very young age, but I don't think that anybody ever truly understands it, no matter how long they live. Organised religion is about power; it is about government, obedience, belief, order, empire, economy, wealth, armies, and maybe especially, ruling classes, thrones and kingship. But it did not start out like that.

In my experience, most people either don't believe in God because they don't believe in organised religion, or they believe quite blindly in the words of the ancient books, and their immature and incomplete approach to almost everything. I know in the days of old, there was a lot that people did not understand about the world and everything in it. I suspect that there is a lot of information that has been deliberately omitted from the narrative, and has not been lost, but used to the advantage of the clergymen, the monarchies, and their empires.

I sense that I have seen the darker side of this metamorphic imperial beast, and the truth in its cavernous and labyrinthine lies, but I can still see the light, and the magic of God.

This manuscript is a collection of my thoughts, broken at times, nonchronological, and disparate, but it is a long story and a complex arc, with deviation and digression at every juncture. I began the story with a collection of letters explaining my more recent frame of mind and what I felt was the correct approach and course of action given the chaotic world events of the past twenty-plus years. It is also the lens through which to interpret most of the writings contained herein, making sense of what are normally perceived as random and seemingly unconnected packets of information. After writing these first letters, I began to realise how much I enjoyed writing and how much easier it can be to place order on chaotic and distressing thoughts, when composed with caution and patience. The more harrowing and painful an idea or belief is to bear, the more difficult it is to communicate it with appropriate articulation, especially when also feeling afraid or distrustful, and experiencing a sense of urgency and panic in the subject matter.

I truly hope that no one is offended by any of the ideas expressed. Most of the present-day events are the continuation of a trajectory that we have inherited from our forebears. If we want a more inclusive and stable world, we will have to face our own mistakes, and more importantly, theirs. Hopefully, our shared belief in God can guide us toward a better and more eclectic future, where together we can build the new empire that will cater to us all.

The stories of humanity, civilisation, and life are not linear stories. They are a collection of meandering, intersecting and diverging paths. I did not write this book with facts and figures or names and dates, but with my wounded heart and inquisitive mind. The human spirit is a complex concept, especially when considering that any being or human spirit could have a continuous and unbroken presence, telling a story not from the perspective of Generals, plutocrats, politicians, or kings, but from the perspective of someone a lot less visible and virtually unacknowledged. I am just a normal guy trying my best to understand this fragmented and endless story of ours. I know that I cannot please everyone, but ideally, I would like help those who need it the most. In some ways, I am still searching for the piece of the puzzle that doesn't fit, and then all of the beliefs I have acquired over the past number of years would come crashing down and through the floor. Somehow, I hope that I

can still find it. For now, I shall try to coexist with this supposedly
new idea of him, and try to understand exactly what that is, because
I, we, and even Mother Earth, need his presence more than ever.

THE DILEMMA

When Prophecy & Circumstance Collide

My name is Khalil Kalifa. I am 43 years old, and I have been struggling with what I believe to be the gift of prophecy.

I have known and believed for over ten years that I am just one very small piece of an undoubtedly vastly extended and unique spiritual and physical presence.

I have been researching the most well-known figures who have been recorded throughout history as having similar experiences. My interest in the stories of people such as the Prophet Daniel, Zarathustra, Joan of Arc, Jesus Christ, Moses, the Buddha, the Vishnu/Hindu avatars, and even the modern American Edgar Cayce have only served to strengthen my belief and instil a greater awareness of exactly what this gift entails and how it has been used – both by him, and those around him.

Given my own experiences with it, I can even find relevance in the stories of seemingly mythological characters such as Apollo (whose birth story is mirrored in the Book of Revelations), Samyaza - Helel Ben Shahar (Book of Enoch), and even Horus of Egypt (whose eye has become, at least in my mind, the symbol of the prophetic gift).

I was born into Christianity, but I would consider myself to be an omnist— a believer in all religions (or elements thereof).

I have recently applied for a visa to visit Iran, as I understand that they are expecting someone like me. I have conducted some limited research on the history of Iran and its unique state religion, Twelver Shia. I do think that they are possibly the only nation prepared to deal with the deeper and broader meaning of what it is that I carry.

I was originally hoping to present myself at the university and explain my situation in great detail. I know that there are extensive learning facilities in Tehran relating to prophetic and religious studies. I believe that I should be surrounded by scribes, scholars, and intellectuals, as opposed to politicians, generals, or capitalist entities and business enterprise. I do understand that all of these authorities are important and can function as extensions of this ability, but it would be better if they could all cooperate rather than compete for control and ownership over the information that a gift like mine can acquire.

I strongly believe that the first credible historical evidence of this gift aligns with the rise of civilisation and empire, along with the origins of religion and the emergence of writing. I suspect that I grasp, at least in part, the true capability of what it is that I possess and what that could mean for society. But I must approach it entirely correctly and with due caution, or it may again fall victim to greed and megalomania and become hidden from us once more.

I was not born into Islam, but I do believe in the true prophethood of Muhammad (PBUH). I have become accustomed to the sense that he is guiding and protecting me. I have also read parts of the history concerning his line of Imams, and their experiences really resonate with me. I know that parts of their stories are deeply tragic and extremely distressing, but they stood for something emblematic and true, carrying forward a tangible legacy for their patriarch. The prolonged power struggle that they were lamentable victims of is truly illustrative of the clash between what Muhammad (PBUH) created and what he left behind. The Imams suffered immensely under the strength of the caliph as it attempted to wrest control over all things Muslim, both material and symbolic.

Recently, I have read a translation and summary of the letter attributed to Abu al-Qassim Muhammad al-Mahdi. It does appear to be authentic and valid in its description of a man wrestling with his immortality and held captive to an eternal battle until its climactic and conclusive conjuncture. I have seen the signs described in its text, and I know that now is the time for something indescribable and virtually immeasurable to be returned to its rightful and true spiritual home.

I have also been reassessing the prophecies of Nostradamus (which I read as a young man), and I am now sure that he has described me, although in an incredibly cryptic fashion. He almost certainly described the British Isles and the nation of Ireland as the birthplace of his prophesied "Chyren Selin." However, Nostradamus tends to use the imagery of ancient namesakes (such as Greek or Roman moon goddesses) in his descriptions, which, if I understand them correctly, are a reference to the end of the Major Occultation in Shia Islam.

I deduce that Selene and Diana were expressed by him to symbolise a full moon, as opposed to the crescent, which I believe to suggest a coming revelation for all believers.

There is so much more, but it is too complex to describe in a single letter. You would really need to be extremely knowledgeable in multiple ancient cultures and their pantheons to comprehend the finer details and deeper meaning of his verses.

I have been quite lost and isolated with these ideas and require intellectual honesty and unfeigned guidance in my spiritual quest to piece together the line of prophets and aid in creating a better and more informed path for global society. I would very much like to communicate, if possible, to all of his tribes a more extensive and inclusive understanding of "him" and hopefully encourage people to repair their relationship with God (ALLAH). I sense that his origins are very deep within our genetics, and that he has almost always been ever-present among us, and in more ways than one.

Finally, and most importantly and urgently, an unjust war has consumed Jerusalem, and there are no signs that it will end on reasonable terms by human action. Israel has become precisely what it claims to oppose, and Palestine must be vindicated. I am not sure that I can change the current political climate or the ongoing international complicity for the injustices that have been committed against the Semitic tribes, but it would be an absolute and unforgivable betrayal if I did not at least try to intervene in some way on the side of truth and justice, especially for those very tribes whom some believe to be his original peoples and their descendants.

My biggest regret is that I did not feel more confident and secure enough in my convictions to come forward and speak out sooner. I have also been a victim of circumstance and subject to far greater machinations than any singular individual would normally be prepared to contend with. The forces that were gathered around me from a very young age were not within the usual realm of expectations, and it has taken a significant portion of my life and mental capacity to fully understand the implications. The only logical conclusion is that some of these bad actors, who have taken pieces of my life as their own, were alerted to my abilities before I was even born. They were coached into taking advantage of my gifts as early and as often as possible and frequently engaged in acts of derogatory sabotage and unrelenting, personalized psychological warfare. I have been mistreated and misled, but I do trust that those closest to me were not the ones who had the authority to enact change; they merely followed the path of least resistance.

It frustrates and upsets me that people chose to follow prophecy and dishonesty rather than approach me openly and honourably. I fear that if we don't tell the truth and face him and ourselves soon, we will descend further into chaos, lies, and barbarism, spiraling uncontrollably toward violence, deception, and obsessive superiority that neither him nor we, will be capable of discerning the truthful reality we all share, and we will become fixated only on furthering our own egotistical misadventures.

We must recognise each other as valued and equal counterparts in this world—different cogs but all unique and extraordinary components in the same great machine.

We were created by an all-powerful and unseen force that has taken billions of years to meticulously construct a progressive organism as complex, unimpaired, and exceptional as each of us are.

I do not want to waste this opportunity to restore lost knowledge and rediscover the wisdoms that we instinctively understood before the advent of modern societal mechanisms such as finance, economy, information collection and control, propaganda, psychological manipulation, and weapons technologies. These have been used to splinter the majority while empowering and enriching a select few, and sometimes (sadly, all too often) serving the self-interest of a single human being.

We are all different for a reason. We can and should be more receptive to that fact, as this is undoubtedly our most redeeming attribute.

Messiah or Mahdi or Prophet?

We have all been waiting for him. Most have been looking for him or at least trying to understand what he is and when he appears. I do think it's fair to say that some have always known when and where he was but have aimed to keep that knowledge for themselves.

The Messiah is merely a reincarnated man who possesses the ability to see the future. He surely lives, dies, and is reborn among every generation since the very beginning. All of his incarnations are connected and interlinked as though they are individual parts of the same mysterious spiritual entity, giving him the ability to see the future of humankind far beyond any single lifetime. This also means that when he passes from death to rebirth, the most advantageous and powerful—yet dangerous—natural ability ever known to man would be possessed by a weak and vulnerable child. This can lead to empires and monarchies, with prior knowledge of prophecy, tracking him down to take advantage and engaging in aggressive actions toward him and/or his people (such as in the cases of Moses or Jesus). But it can also grant him powers of manipulation through knowledge far beyond what any typical child could possess (like, possibly, in the case of Isaac).

I believe that he truly must have been the first lifeform to manifest on this Earth. This is probably the reason why he alone seems to have inherited this godlike ability—akin to a spiritual or genetic wisdom—from our creator that no human being can or should possess, but one always does. This gift, once understood by those around him, appears to have been a large part of the driving force behind the establishment of civilisation and empire, the appearance of religion, and the necessity for writing.

His spirit is somehow linked to genetics. It clearly must manifest among the descendants of his previous forms and is tied to the Y chromosome— making him male virtually all the time.

Currently, he has around 1% Ashkenazi Jewish blood, which, if I understand correctly, is generally thought to consist of approximately 40% Arab Levantine (Iraq, Syria, Palestine/Israel, Lebanon, and Egypt) and 60% South European or Mediterranean (Greek and Italian) mixed ancient blood. It certainly does seem to be true that since records began, he has periodically manifested among the Jews many, many times. And even when he wasn't born a Hebrew, he most likely still carried some of the genes. This implies that men who descend through an unbroken line of Jewish males are the most likely carriers of the messianic gene and potentially the most obvious candidates for the reincarnated prophet to spawn among them.

I have spent over a decade trying to piece together the clues to his existence and understand the knowledge that the books have warned us of. Personally, I feel quite strongly linked to Daniel, Muhammad, and Nostradamus (and possibly Jesus). I am also certain that they have entered into the record certain descriptions that I believe relate to me and the events I have witnessed in my lifetime. I sense a strong urgency in their intentions, accompanied by an overwhelming sense of guilt, sorrow, empathy, and even responsibility for the devastating consequences of some of history's worst man-made events, as well as for the people who have been harmed and those who have brought harm to others.

The past 25 years on Earth have been dominated by chaos, crisis, and a kind of warfare never seen before. These new mechanisms of intelligence, military, politics, finance, and economy can be easily manipulated and are controlled by a small number of people who have the potential to consume the entire world's systems of authority and wealth distribution. Warfare has become so sophisticated that only a few hundred trained personnel are all that's needed to destroy an entire civilisation, practically overnight. The only thing that may hold them back is the financial cost or manufacturing duration of up-to-date weapons and ammunition. Unfortunately, these days, money has become a virtually unlimited resource for the people in control of those authorities, and I fear we have lost touch with the actual cost of our actions. Some politicians are known to condemn violence and encourage peace when the cameras are on while simultaneously authorising weapons sales, supporting aggression, and collecting dividends on their weapon stock portfolios.

When did bombs become an aid to a nation that is withholding food from 2 million people? That food and medicine were donated by humanitarian charities and their sponsors in good faith and belong to the poor, the desperate, and the victims of a war that they did not start but surely have a stake in its outcome.

The rich and powerful have a duty to protect the Earth and all of her people and to guide global society in the right direction—not to sow chaos and destruction with the idea of rewarding themselves and the class immediately above or below them through government contracts or subsidies, inflated share price payouts, or extreme wealth and power. Sadly, modern systems of wealth management and ownership are all too easily manipulated by the upper echelons of global society, who tend to share similar goals and common interests and who benefit from every single human-induced crisis and form of warfare. Wars are clearly a business strategy for certain companies and authoritative figures whose primary motivations are wealth, power, and allies to support them or intimidate others as they pursue aggressive policies and actions. This attitude has become toxic to global society and international integration, preventing us from reaching mutual agreements with fair and honourable outcomes.

We must learn to be content with what we have built and resist the urge to knock everything down and rebuild again just to stimulate the economy, create cash flow through government debt, or enrich the already wealthy. It is dangerous and unconstitutional for the same entities to continue in their quest to possess and control all the world's resources when their only goals are self-serving and megalomaniacal. This system is an insatiable beast, without checks or controls, willing to sacrifice peace, security, lives, knowledge, history, and the environment in its pursuit of dominance and supremacy.

I worry that we have entered into the days that the ancient books warned us about, and I am afraid for us all. We, as a species, have already conquered the Earth, and fighting over whose name or flag will be displayed on its headstone is utterly stale and unproductive. I believe that his gifts can help us assimilate and integrate, but ultimately, he is only one human being and is both unwilling and unable to force people into compliance. The choice can only be made by everyone in society, as he does not want to leave anyone behind. We are all part of his family of extensive tribes. He has no true enemies in this world or the next, as we all belong to the one true God/Allah/Yahweh. I want to share his knowledge with everyone, as this gift belongs to us all and not only links us all together but gives us a direct connection to God, and through Him, to both our ancestors and descendants.

I hope we can all find peace and harmony, learning to accept the world and its natural formations, mechanisms, and inhabitants as they are, and correct ourselves when we do wrong rather than blaming those who we perceive to be our enemies.

I am deeply troubled and concerned about the conflicts between his loyal tribes of tradition. These may be the battles of Gog and Magog that numerous prophets have warned us of, and I would suggest that it is one of those prophecies that has already been fulfilled many times throughout the ages, but each time becoming increasingly destructive. I am not sure if anyone fully comprehends exactly what it means, but I would like to propose that Gog and Magog are brothers, possibly twins, or perhaps even men from the same clan, born generations apart.

Currently, in my mind, it represents the tribes of the same man in different forms. The followers, brothers, and descendants of Moses/Israel, Jesus/Palestine, and Muhammad/Iran are being forced into a conflict of attrition that benefits none of the involved parties. We all need to accept each other as brothers, like Isaac and Ishmael or Romulus and Remus - who became twin empires that should share the world, rather than destroy it in a quest for dominance.

I have been angry, hurt, distressed, and driven mad with this gift, these beliefs, his many tragedies, and forgotten glories. No-one wants to see these recent events play out to an unforgivable and irreparable end. I am still trying to contend with the cruelties committed against Jesus and Daniel, the brutality of the Holocaust, and the ignorance of the Nakba. Now we are starting wars over who deserves the right to possess what is touted to be the only effective deterrent to conflict, genocide, forced regime change, or chaotic and prolonged warfare. I try so hard to nurture the best in us, but it is difficult when, at times, you become only aware of the worst and the permanent scars left behind on our collective human spirit.

The Task

I am a forty-year-old man living in Europe, and I believe myself to be Jesus Christ, the Mahdi. I (details of current form and location) have been referenced in the Book of Daniel and the Book of Revelations, alluded to by Muhammad, and described by Nostradamus, which is why I feel it is important for me to fulfill some of those words and instructions.

Although some of the details in those books are rather specific, I am not quite ready to disclose my current identity. I am confident that I can prove that I have the gift of prophecy and future sight, but it is currently not the right time to use this ability, as these gifts have been misused both in the recent and distant past.

Nowadays, with so many powerful weapons of war and the advent of automated conflict, I fear that deceit and misuse of my gifts could be extremely dangerous—i.e., intelligence warfare, false flags, attempted overpowering of militarised nations, economic warfare, false messianism, aggressive control over financial markets, triggering of violent coups and civil wars, details of future inventions and the people that patent them, and advance knowledge of stock trends and economic activities.

I am interested in publishing some letters or articles explaining to everyone;

- What the Messiah/Mahdi/Prophet is

- My thoughts about the world and its trajectory

- My belief in, and understanding of God/Allah/Yahweh (possibly the most difficult task).

I am not a professional writer, but I do think that I am capable of articulating my thoughts coherently. I have very little trust in the mainstream media, as they are very closely tied to the banks and the post-colonial war machine. To be brutally honest, they would just ignore me if they thought I would expose their media network as part of a privately owned financial system that has taken control of Western democracies. I have no experience with media presentation or public relations methodology.

I worry that almost every corporate entity with significant amounts of money and power has wrested control over every media platform. This leaves me feeling excluded, isolated, and rejected.

No One Can Acknowledge His Truth

20 June 2025

I have recently discovered that I have some Ashkenazi Jewish blood in my DNA, approximately 1%. I now feel that it is even more vital for me to support Palestine in a significant way. I am carrying tremendous guilt and feel partly responsible for their hopelessly cruel existence. I have read so much about the conflict over the past several years, and I empathise deeply with their struggle, especially knowing that they are completely defenceless and without the kind of support they deserve. This past year has been traumatizing, gut-twisting, and mentally unbearable, watching their tragic lives ruled by spiraling brutality.

I have been following your charitable organisation for quite a long time, since before I found out about my Jewish heritage. You are a valued and appreciated voice in the campaign against extreme Zionism, particularly since Zionism has so much influence and completely dominates almost every platform and level of discussion or regulation.

I have never been a massively religious person, but I have always had a strong belief in God. I believe that there are elements within almost every religion that are logically sound and applicable to many things, even science!

I have read the Bible and the Quran, and I have always been quite interested in and fascinated by the prophets and their abilities. They have described the modern world and some of the current events in great detail.

I have known for over ten years that I possess the prophetic gift, and now I know that I am in the male line of Jews—my sisters do not have the Ashkenazi DNA. I am not a Zionist, so I know that my path will not be easy.

Do you think that I should be afraid like Jesus or the Palestinians? I know that most of the victims of the Holocaust were Ashkenazi Jews, and I worry that these events are being administered deliberately by a cult or some kind of multinational "deep state" force in a battle for control over the Messianic bloodlines. I am also from Ireland, so my country and people have experienced two genocides at the hands of the British Empire: the first committed by Oliver Cromwell suppressing revolts in both isles, although he behaved with rampant and unbridled brutality in Ireland, and the second was a purposefully managed famine. I also believe that Palestinians are of mixed Hebrew descent, so I am extremely alarmed by current events: starvation, bombs, and false humanitarianism.

I am not the type of person to seek wealth, power, fame, or glory, but I am unsettled and concerned about the behaviour of some who do. I think that Bush and Netanyahu are some of the most dangerous people of our times, and I worry that religion and racial loyalty are being weaponised and used to mislead the flock.

We have been without a righteous leader for such a long time, if we ever had one at all. The true Messiah really needs to have a voice in this world, and reading or quoting two and three-thousand-year-old books is not bringing us closer to God/Allah/Yahweh. I think we need to evolve, and learning the same things as our ancestors is really only holding us back and encouraging us to follow the wrong people.

I Sound (And Feel) Like a Madman

I wrote to you yesterday, and I am very sure that you have probably assumed that I am either a schizophrenic with delusion and false belief or that I am trying to defraud or hoax you.

I have spent a long time researching and analysing my ideas, and I have never been more convinced of anything in my life.

I would consider this unique and misunderstood prophetic gift, and its implications, to be extremely important and vitally urgent, and not just for my own sake!

Daniel described my phone number, and I do believe that the mark of the beast on the forehead and the hand references knowledge of the future and the ability to act on it, which I can impart to others. But there is more than one beast. The Chiron is a Greek deity and Apollo's adopted son (a semi-primordial being with "inhuman" abilities and presence—referenced by Nostradamus). The other, I believe, to be a cult that arose around this eternally reincarnated prophet in very ancient times (possibly in Sumer or Egypt), that has followed him across the world, tracking the prophetic gift and all of its avatars and becoming a major component of the "everlasting" empire.

Nostradamus called me Chyren (part-beast), Selin (his hometown, suggesting that the new prophet would also be his avatar), Diana (moon goddess and a reference to the end of the Major Occultation in Shia Islam— the arrival of al Mahdi), Thor (my birth name is associated with a hammer), implied the attributes of Ogmios (Celtic deity whose followers are bound to his tongue), and evoked the name of Hercules (king of Rome—Jesus). He also described my birthplace in three different ways, called me an ancient and illustrious monk, and stated that I/he (the Prophet with eternal life) would be crowned by three temporal kings. He also implied that I am twinned with an Angel, like Apollo, Michael, Gabriel, Vishnu, or Horus. This suggested angelic link to the Creator and the Holy Spirit grants him immortality through reincarnation and distinct prophetic ability. He further suggested that this new prophet would share a common thread with five or six other prophets. I believe the most likely candidates are Isaac, Moses, Zarathustra, Daniel, Jesus, Muhammad, Nostradamus, Joan of Arc, and maybe Edgar Cayce. I think that all of these persons are probable or definite avatars of the prophetic gift. I understand that most people would think Nostradamus' verses too vague and cryptic to decipher, but I find the ones I can understand incredibly specific. I downloaded his original verses and translated them using AI just to ensure that I was not mistaken.

Muhammad mentioned my scar/mole and my neither black nor brown curly hair but mostly indicated what it is that I should be trying to achieve. I do not think that I am directly descended from him, but Ashkenazi DNA does contain Levantine blood. Muhammad and the Imams also instructed that their "descendant" would be Abu al-Qassim Muhammad al-Mahdi—like Muhammad but different (carries the prophetic gift)—and would stand side by side with the returned Jesus (they are the same person).

Even the Vishnu/Kalki prophecies describe the future avatar as a man of Indian descent, similar to most or all modern Europeans.

I understand that this is not the most suitable organisation for me to be sharing this kind of information with. Still, I feel I have been rather excluded in a lot of ways because I am neither 100% Jew nor ethnic Muslim, and Christians have been taught to await a godlike man with magical healing abilities who has been unchanged in heaven for the past two millennia. Most of these kinds of beliefs and practices that I describe have been forgotten or, in times gone by, outlawed as heresy and witchcraft.

There is nowhere for me/him to turn unless he is born among those who already have the "right" to claim his legacy as their own.

This Is My Delusion

My dearest Palestine,

I am genuinely sorry for the situation that you face and the political climate that surrounds you. The world has failed in its duty to deliver you from injustice and brutality. The West has become obsessed with its Jewish (Zionist) state, along with its political and economic endgame. It is willing to sacrifice so many of us on the altar of empire to ensure that it can crown itself and govern us all. They have us living in fear and doubt, afraid that the modern world might collapse without the rich and all the wealth they have amassed, or the systems of power that preference their capitalist creations.

Zionism has become the religion of Western oligarchs and their elitist politicians, with greed, glory, and megalomania being their only motivations. They only care for control over the financial system and money creation, as well as dominion over the world's most valuable resources.

Both yours and my blood is among those resources—and traditionally, the most valuable!

The Holocaust never ended; it was merely exported and restricted to another territory. Just as the Nazis targeted European Hebrews, Zionism has targeted the Arab ones. The Nakba has stolen everything from you, although its final solution has been slowed down so as to "plausibly" deny its true goals and purpose.

Just as six million Ashkenazi Hebrews were delivered to the altar of Nazism, and the remains of their bloodlines assimilated and now commanded by Zionism, we too are being robbed and relieved of the chance for him to spawn from among you or for us to spread the messianic blood among their "enemies" and "rivals." Instead, they try to share his blood among royalty and mafia clans in the hope of trapping his spirit and eliminating the threat of him manifesting somewhere they cannot reach or control him. They continually attempt to preemptively destroy any chance of him building an adversarial empire that they cannot manipulate or defeat.

The ruthless and violent have decided that only they are worthy of carrying his blood and possessing his spirit so that they can acquire and abuse his vast knowledge of the future and raise themselves above all other peoples.

The new empire has stolen and hidden his blood for over two thousand years and has truly transformed itself into an insatiable beast. This cult, which rose up around him pre-history, has spent many generations taking control over his many lifetimes, dictating the narrative, using his abilities to build their empire, and creating a network of high-powered spies to take advantage of society. They see him as the ultimate spyware, capable of syphoning valuable information from the future, giving them advanced knowledge of all major events and persons of interest, far ahead of real time.

Daniel warned us of these "imposters," their beast, its network of tentacles, and the synagogue of Satan that has been invisible and silent but growing in might, marching across the earth one territory at a time.

Muhammad called it Dajjal, with only one eye—a reference to the prophetic gift that this monster abuses and craves to retain—along with its associated symbol, and the system of banks it has transformed into, and its blindness to everything but greed and ego.

Nostradamus spoke of the first three antichrists, agents and lieutenants like Napoleon, Hitler, and Bush (Mabus), who committed evil and spread corruption, centralising more and more power and control under a single banner. Sadly, these figures were also said to be replaced by simultaneous antichrists, heralding the return of the great monarch and ornament of the world, Jesus Christ—Mahdi, Messiah, and prophet—who was granted eternal life and cyclical reincarnation by the one true God.

The world's intellectuals were conned into building the world's most powerful weapon. Under the guise of security, defence, and deterrence, even Jews were scare-mongered into pioneering the manufacture of the super-bomb to protect the world's deceitful tyrants. Out of the ashes of World War Two, America and Israel became the world's most well-armed nations, safe from attack while subjugating the world's people, becoming dangerously overpowered, unaccountable, and unafraid of everyone they violently oppress. This system is poisoned by greed, the desire to create gods and kings, and a supposedly divine class of rulers. It has truly deceived the world and all its people, appearing out of control and unrelenting, without a true and just leader or purpose.

They trained an army to steal from a child, abusing the gift of prophecy, and gaining access to knowledge of the future to sow chaos and division. They have placed their own individuals in positions of authority and power, and their tentacles are intent on absorbing all levers and layers of global authority into their network, no matter who or how many they hurt.

I blame the banks; they have become greater than kings, richer than nations, and even more powerful than the empires that created them, usurping authority and wealth, leaving only debt and corruption in their wake. They have turned supposed leaders into puppets and democracy into mere theatre.

They own and administer corporations, weapons companies, global media networks, and an extensive intelligence apparatus to the point where they are now, very obviously, a single entity working in unison. They command most of the world's military and have used mafia, terror networks, cartels, and figureheads, such as Hitler and Bin Laden, to further their agenda and trick the world into blindly supporting and excusing them. These systems of control and influence all behave in synchronicity, no one can stand against them and win.

I am truly sorry, I have failed you, my/his people.

Mahdi

OUR STORY BEGINS

The Blood of the Empire

Civilization, empire, human writing, and mass migration all appear to follow the same historical and geographical patterns. This modern story of advanced human society began its journey in India, spreading out through the Indus Valley and then appearing in Sumer, Egypt, Greece, Persia, Rome, and Jerusalem. Alongside the genetic and archaeological record, these human induced events align clearly with the genesis of world religions and what I believe to be (and what the modern world would come to know as) The Messiah.

The earliest indications of this gifted prophet seem to come from the original Hindu stories of the Vishnu avatars. These stories and supposed early incarnations (fish, turtle, boar, half-human beast or man-lion, and dwarf) are quite ambiguous and open to interpretation—as all or most ancient knowledge was—but are incredibly, and not coincidentally, similar to the story of original life and human evolution. The stories end with Vishnu returning to the heavens and promising to return again in a time of great need in a new form called the Kalki avatar, leaving the Hindu religion foundationally unchanged, yet still ambiguous, for the thousands of years since.

Sumer was, without doubt, the greatest and most advanced civilization of the ancient world, collapsing around 4000 BC. Around this time, some of its most knowledgeable citizenry migrated in two different directions. A large part of the Sumerian migrants, possibly including the priests and upper classes, travelled toward Egypt. Others, such as Abraham—who appeared to follow a more immediate prophecy—settled in what would become Jerusalem.

Egypt/Kemet rose from the Nile Valley as the most fascinating and ambitious civilization to ever leave its mark on history. They built temples, kept extensive records, dominated ancient lands for thousands of years, and constructed the most mysterious and enigmatic stone structures that have ever existed, still drawing awe and wonder to this day. Their multifaceted and detailed religion inspired many other pantheons in surrounding cultures, both near and far. Egyptian society seems to have been dominated by the Amun priesthood, who most likely were the ones who chose—and sometimes deposed—the pharaonic dynasties from within their own ranks. I suspect that these clans probably believed themselves to be the "bloodline of the gods" and made it law that their Pharaoh was worshipped as a god or god-king.

At some stage, their empire became corrupt, dishonest, and massively egotistical. They conspired against their returning prophet, manipulated prophecy, and kept all the power, wealth, and glory for themselves.

Somehow, he eventually became lost to them, or the royal priesthood were simply unable to precisely locate his every incarnation. His presence was no longer required for them to stay in power, and presumably, they had taken precautionary steps to limit the influence of his other clans, safeguarding their own way of life and the unique authority they had over religious identity and sophisticated knowledge. They most likely were attempting to prevent prophecy from being fulfilled while ensuring that no rival empire could rise up around them. It seems they had captured and enslaved their sister tribe and quested to control, corrupt, bribe, or exile their shared prophet.

No-one can be certain exactly how much of the Moses story is factual or accurate, but I do think that it fits with the fall from grace of the ancient Egyptian empire and its ruling classes. Their true "god-king" was born among the slaves and eventually used his gift of foreknowledge to free his own people by manipulating Egypt's royal clergy. Their Pharaoh had become immensely powerful and far beyond the control of the priesthood. There was an uncomfortable yet quiet discontent among them, and so they likely would have chosen to aid Moses through silence and denial, rather than behave as thralls to an ignorant and selfish throne. They had fallen victim to a monster of their own creation (or at least one they had inherited) and their mighty houses were being treated as if they existed solely to extend the king's power. The "Eye of Horus" prophetic gift, symbol of divine rule and providence, had manifested among the enslaved prisoners, or "lesser" peoples, and the royal clans had been exposed as frauds and manipulators. They had existed for thousands of years as the "holy and royal, bloodline of the gods," and without their prophet spawning from within their own powerful tribe, they were doomed to servitude while facing an increasingly angry and hungry public who felt misled and betrayed.

The ruling dynasties had committed themselves to preventing a prophecy from being fulfilled and had enslaved the embryonic "House of David" for over four hundred years. The tribe of "God's Chosen" were about to permanently inherit the coveted line of prophets, and its previous guardians and curators had decided to proactively prevent it's traversal along the branches of his tribal family tree. It seems they had burned themselves by concentrating all political power around a seat of power that no longer respected them. Much like the later Roman Emperors the sitting Pharaoh had become poisoned in his self-belief of being a god, and believed himself far superior to everyone else in his court.

The only viable solution open to them was migration: to follow the Prophet and his new clan to a neighbouring land, assimilate with his tribe to build a new religion and empire, using their honed skills of storytelling, knowledge of empire, insight into prophecy and its source, and their deep understanding of propaganda to control the public mind—appealing to their uneducated psyche and primitive comprehension of history, society, psychology, and God.

Simultaneously, in Jerusalem, Abraham and his companions had set down their roots and became an integral part of the tribal society surrounding the mount which was a focal point of pagan worship. Possibly adopting the idolatrous practices of the localised tribes,

Abraham of Uruk agreed or decided to sacrifice his son Isaac, whom I assume was already known to be the prophesied and returned god king of Sumer (or merely just its principal architect and holy seer). It is plausible that he was feared and maybe blamed for the "apocalypse" that destroyed the greatest human city in the history of the world.

This prophetic gift, or "All-Seeing Eye," gave Isaac the ability to manipulate his would-be executioners; his quiet knowledge of the future and insight into their beliefs and the reasoning behind them, along with the fear of being killed because of false belief and superstition, forced Isaac to bargain for his life, making a promise (12 great nations) that would not be fulfilled until thousands of years in the future. His gift and the spiritual knowledge he possessed surely convinced everyone that no child could possess such vast perception or have the command of an advanced adult mind. The phenomenal event was attributed to an unseen super-being, a truly great God, superior to anything any human mind could ever imagine, design, or comprehend. I honestly think it's also possible that an apparition (the Holy Spirit/Metatron) may have appeared, adding mystery and intrigue, providing proof that such things were not under the control of any "demon child" or half-human deity, or even a man or child of God, further consolidating their newfound belief system.

The Modern Pantheons

Rome and Greece became twin empires with almost identical pantheons. While sometimes the names of their deities might differ, their abilities and purposes remained the same. Apollo and Hercules/Heracles were the most well-known and revered half-human gods in Mediterranean society. Roman culture, in particular, mirrored Egypt, with the (sometimes enforced) belief that their emperor was also a god. It seems that in Rome, at least, Hercules was the epitome of strength, wisdom, justice, and truth, and many self-obsessed emperors tried painfully hard to exemplify him, though usually only superficially, clearly not in personality or reality. Rome was certainly preoccupied with conquering the world, usurping all thrones, and unifying them into a single seat of ultimate power that would forever rule the world.

When Rome invaded and occupied Jerusalem, something unusual happened. Instead of conquering, pillaging, and violently subjugating, basking in victory and ignorance, they quietly studied. They learned about a unique, unified religion that worships just one mysterious God, with no true form, who frequently nominates a wise and holy man to guide, advise, and teach wisdom. This elected seer sometimes issues warnings about the future and our self-destructive behaviors— and carrying the ability of ensuring the preservation of power by foreseeing threats to society and/or its leaders. He had also been recorded as describing visions of a glorious future where this prophet reemerges in a different form and returns to be the crown (and possibly the saviour) of the world empire.

Rome had once again found its Hercules! In killing Jesus, both the Roman Empire and the royal Jewish clergy broke the cycle of the empire's returning prophet and god king (which had become a curse to the ruling clans). They collectively destroyed the beliefs and legacy of the ancient world, while simultaneously ensuring that the path back to power and recognition for him would be extremely difficult, dangerous, and unrewarding. Rome became an indestructible empire "ordained" by God himself, inheriting ultimate power and exacting divine judgment on it's dissenters.

The Jews were the jewel in the empire's crown and its secret weapon, imported as holy and royal "Israelite" blood. Some were welcomed among the elites and royals of the Roman territories, providing access to "divine knowledge" and helping to track the prophetic gift and its hosts. Over time, some became respected intellectuals and business-minded people but were often viewed with suspicion, especially from medieval times onward. They were largely scapegoated during times of social crises and panic, developing unfortunate associations with witchcraft and divine wrath. From the seventeenth century, the Christian empires of Germany, France, and Britain, their banking systems, and public perceptions of conspiracies regarding imperial wars, economic privilege, and social advantage became major issues for most of the lower classes. Jews significantly influenced both sides of this economic divide and helped author new economic models like communism and socialism, which regrettably were often hijacked by tyrants and used as pretexts to seize assets and enforce fascism and despotism.

A MODERN STORY

The Eye of Horus

The Empire of Egypt rose from the Nile Valley in a very primal time. They were likely settled there for thousands of years before constructing their awe-inspiring temples and great stone cities, though few comprehensive explanations exist for their feats of immortality and mind-melting achievements. Considering their primitive writing system but seemingly advanced ideas, there are clearly some significant elements of their history and culture that have been forever lost.

Horus probably never truly existed in a human form, but I am a strong believer in the prophetic gift—the Eye of Horus—which is the ancient symbol of kingship and God's approval. This same gift, which probably came through Vishnu and Gabriel (Jibreel), is what formed the line of prophets that ran through Jerusalem and is also thought to have passed through Iran, and later linking to Muhammad and Nostradamus. Much of the details surrounding this ability has been hidden from the masses, likely to maintain power, stability, and advantage for the ruling classes, and probably out of fear that the small tribes of his most recent incarnations and their descendants may become targets and prisoners of the empire once more.

My knowledge of the Egyptian Pantheon's most well-known characters is minimal, but what I do think is important is their relationships to each other: Osiris, God of the Underworld; his consort Aset or Isis, Queen of the

Throne; and Horus, their human or half-human son. I associate them symbolically with Venus, the Goddess of Love—represented by the evening star ascending into the heavens—and Lucifer, the morning star descending into the darkness of the dawn sky, with their son symbolizing humanity. There is also the idea that these first and last stars of the night sky represent separated lovers searching the heavens and the Earth for each other. Still, the heavens and the Underworld are so vast and ever-changing, that they continue to miss each other as they alternate positions and switch roles in the night sky.

Knowing what it's like to have and use the prophetic gift, I sense that Isis and Osiris resemble Adam and Eve, except they are not human. She is like the Holy Spirit or female archangel, and possibly the mother of the angels— a massless, beautiful creature of light— while he resembles the cold, black darkness of space, personified. I would contemplate that the primordial black matter, completely devoid of light and existing before the Big Bang, could also be a relative form for him. If it was a person or god-like physical form, it might be represented by the Hindu Kali or primordial gods of less specific forms in the Greek pantheon.

The Virgin Birth

In physics, when cold black matter absorbs warm white light, something inexplicable happens. It becomes excited and animated, first absorbing, then slowly dissipating heat and light. Given the right conditions and enough time, this previously inanimate material interacts with surrounding materials—trading heat and electrons, breaking down and reforming—to create the processes needed for the emergence of life. Key factors like pressure, hydration, and a stable environment support the complex chemical reactions required to assemble these new molecules into proteins, the basic components of all living things.

Life will spontaneously manifest at some point when proteins bond together to form longer and more complex chains. Whether that's a seemingly random event in a bustling sea of complex interactions, as energy is passed from one molecule to the next, or if it is simply the inevitable and deliberate consequence of cosmic materials swirling around each other to find order, balance, and their most stable state of energy absorption and release.

That first cellular organism will inevitably split, multiply and colonise, slowly arranging itself into stacks, rows, and columns, evolving and slowly extending its genetic code into progressively more complex and diverse forms. Over billions of years, this process has allowed it to branch out into all of the many forms of life that have existed throughout the ages. All life on this planet is genetically related: trees, birds, fish, whales, lions, and humans. They have all stemmed from that original earthly organism. The scientific name for this first true single-celled lifeform is LUCA, the Last Universal Common Ancestor of all life on Earth – the mother and father of us all.

These scientific processes, when viewed from a spiritual or prehistory perspective, might be represented in the ancient pantheons and religions of all cultures—ambiguous ideas with broad relevance, even in the modern schools of genetics and physics. We are all the descendants of a lifeform that arose from a virgin conception, the meeting of black, lifeless matter and beautiful, warm light. We are the sons of darkness and daughters of light, a form that emerged in the energetic fields generated in the meeting space of these purportedly polar opposites.

These kinds of ambiguous origin tales fit, in a lot of ways, with the story of Adam and Eve, with her coming from his rib like a cell dividing, or the twins Apollo and Artemis/Diana, where he carries the gifts of knowledge and prophecy (and probably represents eternal youth and genetic perfection), and his twin sister is highly skilled in strategies of survival, with strong physical attributes and is easily linked to reproduction. Similar to how complex cells divide long chains of information between their offspring: genders, skills, cellular knowledge, and physical or intellectual advantage.

Maybe basic life is not as primitive or as "brainless" as we might easily presume. Maybe those tiny lifeforms are wiser than we could ever understand or comprehend. They possess incredible intuition and may be more in tune with the multiple dimensions of our reality than we could ever hope to be. The Universe was evidently created and designed with purpose and intelligence. There is an unseen and misunderstood force pushing and pulling things into balance and strategic position. This super-intelligence is woven into the very fabric of our reality and stems from creation itself. It is plausible that it is all part of an invisible spiritual wisdom that governs the universe, transmitting alien blueprints and supreme knowledge, conscientiously and precisely composing layered cosmic devices or complex terrestrial beings, and we will never have the capacity to fully understand its exact origins or ultimate destination.

The Prophet with Eternal Life

My theory about the gift of prophecy is this: The first lifeform was created by an unlimited intellect with immense power and considerate wisdom, coming directly from God, probably through His envoy—the primary Angel and Holy Spirit—whose spirit may be connected to the Earth and the Sun. I imagine she is a Virgin Queen, because she never had a human form or lived a human life, yet she is still the Mother of Life, the Queen of the Heavens, and Earth's sovereign leader.

I sense that she functions as the spirit or soul of the Earth, the "Animus Mundi," a concept from the ancient Greek school of thought. She is the living light that shines upon the world. She appears to embody limitless, kind, and caring rationale which aims to be our guide, loving companion, and spiritual link to The Creator.

I believe she loves all life on Earth and wants us to live in peace and prosperity as long as Earth's systems can support us. This gift was granted to us through her "first son" and can help us extend our time here if we make wise decisions and allow balance, progress, and fairness to prevail. It truly is an extramundane gift sent to us by God with the potential to guide, protect, and save us all.

The New Empire

It is our duty to respect the planet and all of its creatures and be willing to sacrifice comfort and greed to maintain its ecosystems and prevent irreparable damage to our environment. The biggest threat to human life is human society!

The push for needlessly inflated and ever-expanding economies, warring for control over the resources of another land or people, or destroying nature to create false wealth (money) is detrimental to the conditions for life. Every time we kill or take from the earth or its ecosystems, we are slowly poisoning our environment and ourselves, and we are upsetting the natural balance. We were not made to be billionaires; it is a nonsensical concept that attaches make-believe value to a person's worth. No human being could even carry a billion pounds or dollars in its paper form. And the only way you could possibly spend it in a single lifetime is by spending it on others or the world! People and corporations that get rich from oil or rare earth materials are leeching off society. They did not create those materials; the benefits should be shared among society. If we take from the environment and profit from it, we should and must also give back to the world and attempt to restore the once-pristine Earth. The most important concept for society right now should be ensuring that future generations can inherit a fruitful and diverse planet that supports all of God's carefully constructed creatures.

War is killing the planet and is slowly destroying the climate, and some humans are becoming so far removed from the wars that are being enacted. Politicians are pushing buttons and commanding the destruction of faraway lands. Aerial bombardment and remote warfare are an evil of the worst kind, knocking down entire cities and wasting scarce resources that are destructive and polluting to recreate. Inflicting suffering and destroying the means of production and trade, triggering chaos and violence, and paving the way for the worst elements in a society to seize power. In these times, there should be no poor, nor should there be any poor or chaotic semi-failed states, and ordinary people should have a path to seek justice, even against those with authority. Laws are important, most especially for the most powerful and wealthy in any society. After all, they have the means and the ways to commit the worst abuses that affect the largest numbers of people. Mistakes should be rectified, and criminal leaders should face justice.

These methods of human existence is taking away from the most desperate and rewarding ego and corruption, rather than encouraging balance and the tradition of fairness.

Overpowered leaders with limitless military might poison global society and prevent true peace. Wars—especially unjust ones based on lies and false premise—must be outlawed, as they only serve to empower the unworthy, enrich the greedy, and foster corruption within the political class.

No One Should Have The Power To Destroy The World!

We are all extremely concerned that nuclear weapons are being used by tyrants to police the world. This is not about the best system or the most honourable leader winning out in society, but rather about those who cannot be challenged. Threatening nations with weapons like these, or arming unjust allies, does not cultivate true stability and harmony. It enforces dictatorship, ruling through fear, and props up a failed system. There are worrying signs of mafia and oligarchic fascism in the world, and at a level never seen before, which is toxic and menacing to us all. Seizing control of money creation and forcing unserviceable debts on nations is not the way forward. We need to bring ourselves back to reality and let go of immature and unrealistic fantasies. We all belong in this world, deserve peace and security, and must learn to live in equilibrium with the environment and all its inhabitants

THE MOTHER OF ALL SURPRISES

He Is Not Alone

I once had an indescribable experience of being taken to heaven by the hand of a beautiful and youthful female spirit. I believe I was around seven years old and being placed under unnecessary stress and pressure. I was being interrogated and hypnosis was being used as a strategy to reshape my mind, forcefully extract information, and coerce me into agreeing to do things that I would never want to do. I was isolated, sleep-deprived, and truly felt like I was losing my mind.

Then it happened. As I covered my eyes and almost cried out with emotional stress and overwhelming anguish, something physical quickly and firmly grabbed my hand, as if to catch me from falling. I felt a beam of fast-moving light and energy move through me from my head to my feet, transporting me somewhere no human being could willingly choose to go. Suddenly, I was standing in a room that resembled the Temple or Palace of Olympus, the home and throne of Zeus. Grey and blue marble pillars with swirls of white and flecks of yellow surrounded a large room with open walls and ceiling, and at its centre was a strikingly ancient-looking oval-shaped wooden table. The table was a dark, dusty brown, neither polished nor carved with intricate symbols. It looked bare and untreated, split and over-dried, while worn and eroded across its top.

I imagine it would have felt rough to the touch, as it appeared to be unfinished and unsmoothed at the joints, corners, and edges.

The Council of Heaven

There were human-like figures all around the table, which seemed to take up most of the space in the room. I was standing back from it, but there was a gap in the crowd in front of me. As soon as I appeared, she became aware of me. She was standing by the table to my left, conversing with some silhouettes who may have been dressed in hooded robes. Immediately, she turned toward me, crossed the room, knelt down, and embraced me in a single, smooth, graceful motion. I sensed her mind and heard her voice, which seemed to sing to me, but not in any human language, and I felt her firm, purposeful embrace.

I was hurting, in pain, and felt betrayed and unloved, but she healed me. She communicated with my deepest self just by touch and instantaneously showed me parts of my future. She was tall and felt strong, so beautiful and kind, loving and considerate, but also seemed very ancient and immensely powerful. She appeared blonde and fair and may have worn a long grey dress that was rough and heavy like tweed, with a blue corset and white on the shoulders. She seemed slightly aged and weathered, even battle-hardened, but still gentle and intuitive—a true warrior queen. She was unchanged by the trauma of destruction and the inescapable awareness of looming annihilation. This place seemed so alien and far away, yet still very much connected to, and aware of, human experience and struggle.

There was quite a lot of commotion when I entered, almost like a war room that had been strategically attempting to deal with the repercussions of a challenging security alert.

I asked her about God, but she gracefully gestured toward the head of the table to my right. There were figures almost blocking my view, but I could see there was no one or no-thing there—just the gaps between the great marble pillars, showing the deep, black, infinite sea that surrounded the heavens. I couldn't see any stars or the Earth, just boundless, indistinguishable black. It almost seemed to be animated and alive, but invisibly chaotic and silently destructive. I did not fully understand and became confused, but before I could ask more difficult questions, she gestured again to my right, almost directly beside me. There was a young man, maybe 25 or 30, noble and masculine, yet slim and athletic. He wore a brown robe or toga from his shoulders to his knees. His hair was midlength, brown, and curly, and he wore a golden laurel wreath with golden leaves and interwoven stems. In his left hand, and tucked into his hip by his elbow, right by my eye level, was what seemed to be a clay or stone tablet, with scrolls and pages bound to it's front by a narrow red ribbon! I looked up to observe his face; he was on my right, facing the table, smiling, and watching me from the corner of his eye. He seemed to be acknowledging his awareness of me. I immediately knew he could only be Apollo, the angel or deity of knowledge and prophecy. It almost seemed as if there was something vaguely familiar between us—like we were mirrored in an obscure sort of way, or maybe comparable to twins from very different times, and very different mothers.

If he was what he seemed—an angel with godly knowledge and prophetic ability—then the tall lady who hugged me with the kind of care and compassion that could only have come from God or Heaven - that might possibly be his mother. Possibly even Mother Earth or Mother Nature, personified. If he were her son, he would likely represent the first lifeform on Earth, immortal through reincarnation and eternally in his prime.

He records all human knowledge and can show us the future, helping us acquire the knowledge of the angels and maybe even universal laws and alien blueprints, like Noah's Ark, the Tower of Babel, or the Ark of the Covenant. He might help us to understand complex ideas granting wisdom far beyond our years. He could potentially guide and save us from our own blind mistakes and misused knowledge, helping us advance faster and further than all the other lifeforms under her care. He appears to represent genetic perfection, eternal youth, wisdom, and forward-planning—the sum of all human knowledge and the desire to build and become advanced technologically, physically, psychologically, and socially. I wonder if he truly was the first of us—the single cell that designed and built the natural world, populating it to its pinnacle. Was he aware, in the deepest spiritual sense, all the way back then, how the aeons would transpire or even how it all might end?

My time was almost up, and I took one more glance around the room. Across from me, on the other side of the table, I saw Mary and Joseph sitting on a bench that ran perpendicular to the table, facing its head—where God should have been. She looked so young, wearing a hijab, dressed mostly in white and pale blue, and was crying. Joseph sat beside her, his arm cradling her shoulder, comforting her.

I suspect her tears signified resistance to Christianity taking her image and replacing the meaning behind the apparitions and supernatural phenomena that should have been attributed to the Holy Spirit, God's Envoy and Queen of the Angels, who paid me so much attention and care, providing guidance and renewing my inner peace as I stood in a sea of turmoil and conspiracy. I would guess the immaculate conception is actually untrue, and that early teen Mary was probably raped by a Roman soldier and even sold into slavery—purchased and rescued by Joseph, who was maybe twice her age. Although I am sure that if the Envoy chose to appear as Mary, mother of Jesus, she certainly could have taken that form, especially if it symbolized or signified a part of her message.

As I looked all the way around the table on the opposite side toward its foot to my left, the figures gathered around it seemed to trail off into silhouettes, and may have even begun to take forms that were becoming less and less human, until they became further and further away, vanishing into the distance. I was back to where I started, still angry and upset with those around me, but willing to ignore their ignorance and repress uncomfortable memories and ugly truths until the time was right to piece it all back together.

The Hand of God

There was still one detail that did not quite fit with the memory of my experience. I suspected that the girl who grabbed my hand was not the angel who hugged me. The hand that latched onto mine felt petite and soft—a much smaller frame than the Queen in heaven. I could vividly picture a much younger, smaller, and thinner figure than the giant who had to kneel and crouch to cradle me. This second lady may have been so graceful that she was silent, and so gentle that she never spoke. I imagined a girl not quite as fair as the Queen, but with curly hair so long it became like a cloak. She seemed to fly without touching the ground, gliding in to reach down from above, instantaneously lifting me up. I could envision someone so tiny and youthful that she may not have seemed much older or bigger than me.

I have thought deeply about that moment; it was fleeting and accelerated but has lasted an eternity in my mind. It is difficult to be fully confident in some of the details, even though they are all so clear—especially the hand that suddenly reached for me with strength and purpose, like it caught me and saved me from a high fall, right at that most decisive moment.

I believe that my anomalous experience could align quite neatly with the stories of the Celtic goddess Oona. She has been described as a nymph who personifies the ancient Irish woodlands. However, she is also identified as a fairy queen who blends with the natural environment, being invisible most of the time. She is a designated protector of all living things, especially young animals, and can move silently through the forest to avoid detection. Her name is also similar to the Irish word for "lamb" (uan).

I had my doubts, but it is not easy to deny the similarities between my experience—something I could never have seen—and the descriptions of her in Irish mythology. I just felt the unexpected physical grasp of a small, gentle, but strong hand.

At first, I thought she might have been the angel's daughter or a relative form for Mother Nature when the earth was young and life was at its most tranquil. But they each appeared unique and played very different roles in my deeply enthralling experience.

I cannot fully explain any part of my experience. I never would have thought I could believe in things such as angels or nature spirits. I also think, at that exact moment, it may have been precisely what I needed to weather the storm and to someday, make landfall once more, speaking of exotic gifts from a faraway world.

I do wish those things had not happened. I worry that some of those involved in distressing me may have deliberately hurt me to in an attempt provoke the supernatural. I definitely do not think it is something I can invite or cause at will. I did not even pray or ask for help in that moment—I was too mentally frustrated and hurt to think clearly or calmly. I cannot even be sure why I was being treated that way, but I also believe that if I were not a child drowning in conspiracy and smothered with lies, those beautiful spirits would not have intervened to bring me healing and spiritual renewal.

THE GLORY OF GOD

No one can be sure exactly what God is or how He came to be. He possesses ultimate power, infinite knowledge, omnipresence, and eternal immortality. He has existed since before the universe and will certainly outlive its current incarnation and the many that will come after. He will conclusively destroy this version of the world, collecting all the materials, energy, and information it contains, recombining them, ultimately sparking the cycle of creation once more. I have spent much time contemplating the fabric that threads this universe and all that dwells within.

I have countless questions about what may lie outside the dimensions of our known and unknown world, if anything at all. I wonder if God has any true form, considering He is both every form and formless. He is definitely an alien—something so alien that no human mind could ever truly comprehend His nature, intent, or true, raw spirit. He is all-aware but exhibits a good-natured purpose and understands the moral dilemma of being human: animal-like, killing to eat, committing sin to amuse and occupy oneself, fighting violent battles of survival or greed, and struggling against one's own nature, or the nature of others. I believe He sends us knowledge and guidance and has elected certain people who consistently and intuitively want what is best for all His creatures, and even for the Earth itself. Prophets and Messiahs have served to teach us a better way and encourage us to respect each other, taking care and diligence to inspire our laws and teaching us how to think and behave. This proves that God truly is a moral authority, perfect in virtue and principle, but simultaneously demonstrates that we are not. Without His elected communicators, we would probably be lost. Many understand the same universal logic, but without supernatural ability and "proof of God," we might ignore their ideas and continue into the abyss of animalistic violence and unflinching cruelty.

I often ponder the possibility that our universe is alive and conscious—an all-encompassing biological, mechanical, numerical, energy and information-based organism that lives, dies, and is reborn, remodeling itself into order, balance, and harmony from the chaos of its conception. If this hypothesis is true—and I believe it is logically sound—that organism would be God. It spends infinity fusing and processing matter into information, massless energy, airy particles, and heavy or dense metallic substances, sometimes spreading those materials far and wide to be remade into other, less energetic objects of much lower entropy. Often, these substances slowly stitch together to create life that further breaks down its environment to harness materials and maximise potential by constructing organic and botanical forms or consuming and splitting molecules to evolve and extend their genetic code, or fashioning colonies of cells into structures that function as biological appendages and organs.

It's almost as if the frequency of motion and the transfer of energy throughout the cosmos is spacetime acting as a medium for transmitting information and cosmic blueprints from seemingly inanimate but ever-changing entities to more dispersed components. This system allows these new elements to establish themselves as conscious beings that intricately work together to fabricate even more elaborate forms. I can't help but wonder if this interaction of virtually everything in the heavens means almost every atom or molecule in the universe has the potential to evolve into part of a conscious lifeform with unlimited connection and unrealised capability.

Maybe if these individual particles were ever part of a living organism in any one of the universe's infinities—in this fascinating macrocosm—they always were and forever will be spiritually conscious, aware, and extremely intuitive. Perhaps these human forms we have taken were purposefully manufactured for us to observe, measure, and record, storing information for the Father of the Cosmos. Without conscious life to observe, this universe technically would never have existed; conscious life is a necessary part of its reality. For atoms and particles to find order and obey patterns, they must be observed—and the universe is possibly just a larger example of that.

If the universe develops and behaves like a computer program—a binary code (protons and electrons)—manufacturing increasingly complex chains of code (blueprints and materials), and eventually heavy matter from the same basic components fused and energised, and ultimately spread or absorbed into a super-dense and indestructible object, could that mean, just like an AI program generating, consuming, and assimilating expansive amounts of data, this universe could have the potential to become self-aware and independent? Inevitably, even more conscious and aware than the organisms it strives to create?

The universe follows a pattern, a code, sets of rules and laws, probably starting from the same state it will finish, before beginning anew. It is superintelligent, constantly evolving, and self-designed with purpose and intent—that can only mean it is aware, alive, and aims to find balance and order. Even in the face of complete chaos and utter destruction, it reforms, heals, cools, spreads, and creates a home for the life it chooses to create.

The universe is a very strange and indescribable object. It almost certainly hyper-rotates: from interior to exterior, then alternates again. It lives for three infinities: creation and balance, death and destruction, contraction and rebirth. Two of these phases we tiny humans may never understand, simply because they exist far outside our limited reality. Those terminal states are not subject to the normal rules and laws that it has taken us so long to figure out—and now we cannot imagine any world without those stipulations.

Judgement

The simplest and most basic form for me to imagine this kind of God is the seemingly singular dimension that existed before the moment of creation: an "infinitely" dense point of immeasurable forces that has reabsorbed and reconfigured all the information and energy from its previous states, now so compacted and compressed that space or time cannot exist. It's hard to imagine that this object could rotate or resonate, but I would guess that if it did ever manage to rest or find its lowest state of entropy, it would become so overloaded with energy and compressed mass that it would surely explode—or implode—or both at the same time. And all the forces contained within, having being crushed to their maximum degree would only rebound, all at once.

There was a time when I felt so afraid thinking of God in this form: cold and black, without light, all-knowing, all-seeing, all-consuming,guide-present, alien and unfamiliar—eternal death and darkness. I felt only fear and panic, overwhelmed and overburdened with despair and internal chaos.

I was aware only of the inescapable, unavoidable draw of its crushing power, helpless and alone when faced with its dominance and preeminence. A genderless beast devoid of any human emotion, with only mechanical and thoughtless logic.

This monstrosity seems like the true alpha and omega—the beginning and the end—of time and our universe. It has an absolutely beastly presence, but oddly does not possess a beastly nature. It exists outside of time and space but is strangely still eternal, omnipotent, and ubiquitous. The very fabric of spacetime is inseparable from this colossal behemoth. An immeasurable force with infinite reach, and there is no escaping its presence or denying it's truth.

I found these ideas frightening, difficult to accept, and even harder to understand but somewhere along this journey through life and knowledge, we will have to accept the mystery of God and all of His forms and their uncomfortable ramifications. He will always be outside of our limited human capacity but always aware of, and empathetic to, our nanoscopic will. He truly is a wonder, inspiring awe and humility. If God did not exist, we would not exist. This universe would not exist. Nothing could exist without His inordinate presence that consumes and recreates all in continuance and permanence.

UNCOMFORTABLE TRUTHS

Alone

The first time I was hypnotized, I was five years old. I became immediately angry and spoke like a man, probably sounding a lot like a demon who possessed the body of a child. I knew I was being conspired against and betrayed by my closest kin.

This probably happened multiple times by the age of seven when I was visited by an entity that I would eventually come to associate with Orpheus or Morpheus—the formless holy spirit from Greek mythology. It is said that it visits great leaders and persons of notable social significance, offering counsel and guidance, taking symbolic forms that express intention and familiarity. I suspect this spirit does not always communicate directly using human language but signifies a complex device of divine will and guidance. In my experience direct instruction aimed at specific actions is generally not their directive. We have been given free will, awareness, and knowledge beyond our years. Yet one altruistic human can easily be overpowered and defeated by the many others surrounding them. I received healing, inner peace, a sense of enlightenment, and possibly a seal on some of the abilities and information I held inside.

She saved my mind from deliberate ignorance, cruelty, and sabotage, and the kind of warfare enemies employ when they pretend to be friends and allies. This spirit did not seem human. I got the impression she was more likely to be an extensive spiritual presence or higher consciousness, watching us closely and likely inhabiting the Earth rather than ever walking upon it. I know how ridiculous this seems, and it has taken me quite some time to understand the meaning but the great and mighty spirit that visited me had taken a form of resemblance to Cate Blanchett's character, Galadriel, from the original Lord of the Rings film trilogy. This happened to me in 1989, over a decade before those films were made and long before that actress became a familiar face to most people. However, I did not remember this strange event until 2011 when I rediscovered many of the truths that had been hidden from me.

The more I think about it, the more sense it makes. I was like Frodo—weak, small, good-natured, but carrying a great darkness and surrounded by uncontrollable evil. I possessed a power so superior and commanding— capable of conquering the world, uniting many tribes, and changing people's minds that it turned most of those around me into Golum-like creatures, seduced by the ideas of vast wealth, ultimate power, unlimited influence, and being the centrepiece of the world's envy and idolatry. She was beautiful and kind, gentle and thoughtful, telepathic and empathetic, expressing altruistic intention, and intervening only because she deemed it absolutely necessary. This gift is my burden, and I am alone with it, but she protected me long enough for me to become mentally and emotionally independent. She was tall, like the Nephilim, and Gandalf, possibly dressed similarly from the waist down. She showed me deeply symbolic places, figures and a great dark force implying a form for the One True God—a raw, calculating sea of invisible energy, aware of itself and its power but unable to stop or slow down along the path to its inevitable destination, taking us all with it. I sensed even she was afraid but at peace whatever that may mean. I was confused, and it took me quite a long time to analyse the symbolism and suggestion behind that alien encounter.

The universe seems like a mechanical device, like a clock winding up then winding back down. It is self-aware, containing copious amounts of information, with creation, expansion, fusion, compaction, and destruction as part of an endlessly repeating cycle. Possibly even like a computer program that changes the code slightly with each cycle, learning and becoming more omniscient, playing out all possible scenarios and using many different parameters—as if testing us and itself, fulfilling all possible objectives, expanding into each possible dimension and exploring every alternate reality. It has no equal, rival, or enemy; it is unique, almighty, and alone in its purpose. She seemed like his companion or consort and messenger, but I wonder if there are more like her in that deep, unending world of worlds.

We believe the Messiah comes from God, possibly indirectly, still possessing some of His raw ability to manipulate time—showing us the future, siphoning valuable knowledge, helping us prepare and progress, and sometimes warning against our unchecked nature. Considering this man, this "gift of prophecy," is always among us, it stands to reason there must be one on every life-giving world, as part of the force guiding consciousness toward its ultimate destiny or accelerating the journey to knowledge and awareness—ensuring we understand ourselves and become aware of God's purpose in this limited window of existence. If we are God's eyes and part of His mind, the more we learn, the more He learns. The more we observe, measure, and record, the more aware He becomes of Himself, and perhaps in the next loop in the lifecycle of the universe, we will learn and evolve even faster.

The Curse of Knowledge

The desire to own, control, and become the apex of our own species—the dominant alpha—is a dangerous instinct. It is part of the genetic proclivity that drives all life forward and ensures survival, but the more powerful a species becomes, the more inevitable it is that this inclination changes into its own greatest threat.

The greatest threat to any species is the risk of drastically changing its own environment. Without other populous species to process its waste, it will slowly poison itself.

Humans are the most successful organisms in the known universe—so successful that we have changed the entire world and nearly outnumber all other species combined. We have bulldozed forests and drained rivers dry. I believe we need to synchronize with our environment and better plan our populations. We must preserve and create more wildlands and allow the oceans to regenerate. Life was once abundant on this world, but the more we multiply and exploit our surroundings, the more we degrade our home. We should behave more like we are merely a necessary function of the Earth and not believe that we are its masters. If we were its true masters, we would respect and preserve the planet and aid its quest to blanket the world with all diverse forms of life.

A Prophet in the House of Thieves

When I was around ten, I was sent to summer classes once a week on Saturdays to learn karate. The club was run by mafia and terrorist types protected by local guards. They used it as a front to build gangs and control children's lives indefinitely. It also formed part of an elaborate plot to lure the young Messiah into a trap, intending to abuse his prophetic gift and ensure that everyone around him would aid in that deceptive operation, rather than hinder it. I had already been primed for shock induction (hypnosis without knowledge or permission) since I was five. The coach could walk behind me, snap his fingers, and I would suddenly enter a trance. While under, I knew what I could do—it was just who or what I was. I was unimpressed by how I was being treated, and I did not try to hide it.

This situation went on for ten weeks, each summer, for two years. He would ask me questions about the future, sometimes asking me to do things like have children with them, try to bribe me, or ask for my lifetime loyalty. It's difficult to describe the contradiction of that situation—being hypnotised and interrogated, being threatened with violence and mutilation, being told that my life, health, and even my looks would be ruined deliberately and permanently, or that I and my children would be bullied and abused for life, and that these mafia-oriented gangs would mark families and exact revenge on the easiest targets available to them (if anyone got in their way)—but still, I felt so far outside of my own body, almost as if I was someone much older, half-conscious and watching those events unfold through the tunnel of someone else's mind. I was unafraid and unwilling to help them, promising I would never agree. He seemed unhinged and dangerous and tried many times to engage in a power struggle with me, which I tried to ignore.

He was attempting to induct me into a cult, to brainwash and control me, and force me to allow someone else to decide my thoughts and feelings. He asked me to make them "great," rich with political might, and to turn them into a class of people more powerful than the nation we inhabit. He threatened murder and mutilation against anyone who sided with me, spoke of bombs and mass murder as if it were his way of praying, and even called himself the beast. They were already aware that I was the Messianic Prophet reborn. They already knew some things about the future and asked me about some of the worst events yet to come, like 9/11 and the flight simulation training equipment that was purchased in Britain, delivered to Ireland, and smuggled to Afghanistan.

He asked me about Israel and threatened me when I said that we need to help Palestine. He may have suggested that such gangs and terrorists were working with Western intelligence agencies and were rewarded with impunity, social advantage, wealth, and corruption for their cooperation. Some of these gangs were even used as a pool to source civil service employees whose loyalty was not to their own country or its citizenry.

I tried not to give away too much information, and I was aware that I would be unable to stop the coming events and the wars they would trigger. I was just one person pitted against a private army and a network of corruption that encircles the globe, like the tentacles of a parasite that has attached itself to the face of humankind.

The Beast Who Deceived The World

I can only assume that we have reached the part of the ancient book that warned us of the great dragon that would try to consume the world, die a dramatic death, and rise again to chase the woman about to give birth. It would have seven heads and ten crowns, which I believe refers to the empires, nations, and crowns it has passed through on its journey from ancient times into the present. It has usurped many seats of power and destroyed the rest. Its number is 666, and you cannot buy or sell without its mark. It could only be the private banking system! More wealthy and powerful than any nation, it has seized the world's resources and the means of money creation to reward itself and its supporters.

Crisis banking was born in 1666 after the Great Fire of London. Money created by the private banking system was loaned to the government to rebuild the city, and was paid back through taxation, birthing the system we still use today. This banking system began in Germany and was subsequently adopted in Britain and France. These imperial banks were owned by the same families who descended from the original German clan. This banking cartel has only expanded since, financing wars and amassing wealth through slavery and colonization. Since it conquered the American financial system in 1913, funded and won two world wars, its influence has only grown, intent on funneling all the world's resources through its own ministries.

Since the EU transformed into a superstate and centralized control of the monetary system, we have been dominated by eternal crisis, debt, conflict, austerity, and borrowing—and now the attempt to turn Europe into a military superpower, with total control being given to whoever the bankers nominate. The infamous "King of Terror" from the Nostradamus prophecies may have actually been a reference to the ratification of various EU treaties that solidified its single currency. This centralization of power and unified control over financial markets set the stage for the consolidation of global finance, enhancing some major system flaws in the process, inflating markets in the aftermath of 9/11, and subsequently crashing the global economy. Private agencies then purchased large portions of working-class wealth under the guise of "economic rescue packages," facilitating the largest transfer of wealth in history. They redirected trillions in assets to private capital management agencies, investment funds, and equity groups, earning the name "Vulture

Funds" and becoming the biggest landlord agencies worldwide overnight!

Before 9/11, all these actions were illegal—along with hedge funds. This kind of economic behaviour of selling high-risk loans and marketing them as valuable stock in trading companies to feed demand in the stock market is what triggered the Great Depression in 1929. New economic laws were introduced to limit such destructive and reckless behaviors.

All these laws were abolished in 2001 as part of George Bush's "economic stimulus packages" when "terrorists attacked our economy" because "they hate us for our freedom." This oversimplification is huge, especially since it was the American government and Western intelligence networks that created the Al Qaeda network. Bush then went to war against countries previously used as proxies against the USSR and Iran, spreading chaos and instability among every nation that was not fully aligned with the Western banking cartels' interests.

The Bush Administration (Mabus? Bush Ad-Min!), was possibly the most blatantly corrupt in American history. I fear they may have allowed an attack to justify war and dismantle financial regulations, then cooked and crashed the world economy, framed Iraq for weapons of mass destruction, and possibly allowed the failure of an oil rig. Vice President Cheney's chemical company made over 40 billion from the Gulf cleanup using a newly created chemical that can disperse oil molecules in water. Not to mention suspicions around three collapsed buildings, the unlikely plane crash scenario at the Pentagon, the missing $2 trillion at the Pentagon on September 10th, unusual stock market activity before the attack, and cancelled investigations into Wall Street trading, which were deemed too threatening to the delicate economy.

The Bush years were possibly the most destructive period in world political history: chaos, propaganda, destruction, international policies of torture and psychological experimentation, preventable disasters, the largest marine oil spill in history, illegal war on false premise, a bottomless money pit in the Afghanistan war, constant terror alerts and fearmongering, extreme debt, market inflation, economic collapse, and a borderless "war on terror." It was difficult to keep track of all crises during those years, and it never let up at all. It was almost as if the architects of the intelligence coups that were triggered abroad had decided to usurp power at home, but to do so, they had to fool the entire world.

This series of man-made events also resulted in the largest wealth creation period in history. However, this new wealth was mainly created as debt, described as "bailout packages," literally handed out as virtual blank cheques to the richest and most powerful corporate entities on Earth.

The Carlyle Group—the richest private equity firm at the time, conglomerating over 300 companies, and mostly run by ex-CIA personnel with the Bush's holding a controlling share—divided Iraq and awarded themselves most of the new government's private contracts. An incredibly dangerous precedent was set.

The Walker Bush clan were bankers after all. Prescott Bush married into the Walker banking dynasty and fronted a bank in Switzerland before World War Two, funneling approximately $200 million back to America when the war was over. Most likely, this money was made during various business ties between various European and American companies, the Nazi economy, and its aggressive war machine.

I am highly concerned that a dangerously corrupt bank, along with its extensive global intelligence network, which seizes and divides foreign assets, spreads corruption and debt strives to create and enrich a bourgeoisie class to keep them in power. Such a system would weaken democracies, influence elections, and force everyone to serve their dishonest agenda.

Financial patterns and climactic events since 2001 have played out like an elaborate Ponzi scheme, creating a billionaire underclass of speculators who are tied to the banks and intelligence agencies. It seems as though there was a concerted effort to rush toward late-stage capitalism, where new financial classes consume and assimilate everything as part of a privately owned capitalist empire. Global democracies, housing, healthcare, and education are now controlled, owned, or heavily influenced by the ultra-rich, whose interests are antithetical to the purpose of the economy, or government autonomy and independence.

The Signs of Ad Dajjal

Obama stormed into power on the platform of change. People were desperate to escape the chaos and manipulation of the Bush era. He immediately set out to rescue the collapsing financial system. It was so well-timed it appeared orchestrated, and as Bush bowed out, the new President borrowed 16 trillion from the banks to save the banks. He also may have directly or indirectly facilitated the rise of ISIS, spreading the chaos from Iraq and violently overthrowing the governments of Syria and Libya in decades-long civil wars that still rage on.

I worry that Western democracies have become mere servants and puppets for the banks. They control more wealth than any group of nations, especially when you consider that nations' own debt and their capitalist classes own the material wealth. They have the power to use terrorism and false flags to achieve their objectives. They control a global intelligence apparatus along with most media networks and can trigger wars or overthrow nations practically overnight. No one can oppose them. They decide who is placed in power, who is allowed to acquire nuclear weapons, and who gets overthrown when they've served their purpose.

My biggest fear is that they are also obsessed with the messianic bloodlines and they are willing to kill all that they cannot corrupt. In Nazi Germany, certain forces were trying to force the Jews to Palestine to conquer the territory violently; those who refused had their wealth confiscated, and they were sent to the camps. Few survived, but it may just be that they kept certain people (orphans and lone survivors of their families) from each of the ancient bloodlines alive, in the hope of controlling all the clans under Zionism, and of birthing a new Messianic line of prophets. These patterns of violence, manipulation, and control do resemble an occult practice (which the Nazis were known for), but maybe isn't all that different from how Pharaoh or Herod behaved when they targeted the firstborns from every family or imprisoned the tribe who would spawn a new line of prophets.

For thousands of years, there have been classes and clans obsessed with making sure that he can only come from them. And if, generally speaking, he can only return among his own descendants, or the descendants of his previous avatars, they only have to make sure that he either does not have any offspring, or that he can only have children with them. But this will only work as long as the tribe is small.

Hitler was obsessed with the Jews and the Messiah, famously calling himself the German Messiah and attempted to convince society that he was the second coming of Jesus Christ. I find it impossible to believe his only motivation was racism. It is a very dark and murky period in history, and would be difficult for me to understand anyone's motivation for such heinously destructive cruelty and gleeful psychopathy. But given my experiences and unique perspective, I am genuinely suspicious, considering the potential worth of permanently capturing the prophet's spirit (through his clan) and exploiting his gift eternally. There should be at least fifty or a hundred million Jews in the world today. I am disturbed and distressed by the actions inflicted upon them and their unification into a device that continues the imperialist ambitions of Rome, the European Monarchies, and the American capitalist empire.

Hypothetically, if the Holocaust was part of an elaborate, multi-generational form of psychological warfare, then they also managed to trick the world's intellectuals into building them the weapon that would rule the world. Out of fear and sorrow for their own people, and dread that this "enemy of humanity" would obtain the nuclear weapon first, the most intelligent individuals of many nations submitted to generals and politicians—people they normally distrusted—and joined the quest to build the "super-bomb," sealing the fate of the world for generations.

The brutal Nazi war machine also smashed down most of Europe's borders, ultimately reforming it into the unified economic and currency zone that it is today.

The legacy of Bin Laden has also had a similar effect and is still playing out across the Middle East. It seems the West has eagerly taken advantage of the opportunity to overthrow every non-ally in the region, with tragic consequences.

Chyren / Chiron

Even if this idea about the driving forces behind these events is wrong and I am misunderstanding the motivations, or just stating what it might look like from an aerial view, unbroken narrative or an oversimplified historical account, and if I have become traumatized by historical guilt, I still believe someone knew the future through ambushing the messianic gift for the many centuries since these events seem to have been set into motion.

The Prophet/Messiah/Mahdi is a beast because of his inhuman gift (but he obviously wants to use it for the betterment of us all). He can see the future far beyond his own lifetime through the eyes of the next in line. He would inevitably give away his next identity to his would-be captors under interrogation, who share the information with their cultist allies.

So, if they knew, they either chose to allow it to happen or planned for the outcome, or they conspired to set these events in motion, increasing their power and wealth on both sides of the equation.

I think that the ancient folk around him saw this apocalyptic future. They foresaw a beast who would become its own twin, almost as if it faked its own death and feigned a conclusive defeat. They described impostors from the synagogue of Satan. Some verses describe Jerusalem as being destroyed and littered with the bodies of the faithful, conquered by the ancient values of Sodom and Egypt, and suggested it would have to be rebuilt and possibly remade by God itself.

The Cult of Conspiracy and Corruption

For quite a few years I was trapped in a mental battle with the delayed recollection of the memories from when I was five, seven and ten. I was traumatised, feeling like I was brainwashed by terrorists and mass murderers, while they engaged in conspiracy and corruption. My mind was not my own anymore. I was being poisoned by someone else's thoughts and desires, centred around abuses and murder, and stealing pieces of other people's lives for themselves, to wear like jewelry. These people were obsessed with image and reputation, and the sly, sneaky ways to get the better of someone. In their minds, proving themselves to be greater, superintelligent, and supreme. They were calling themselves "alphas" who were "vying for supremacy," while they ganged up to bully a kid and employed children to harass and abuse me in their place. They bragged about murder, bombs, and disappearing while being protected by their clans, gangs, and their spies with power and authority.

They were completely seduced by the idea of royalty and wealth and were engaged in a mafia-oriented class war to ensure only themselves or their underlings could succeed in the higher levels of society. They were fixated on holy blood and prostituting themselves for power, money, impunity, and glory.

I loathed being the centre of that type of attention and was repulsed by their delusions of grandiosity. They would never accept less than what they demanded. I truly felt like a victim of MK Ultra, but these people seemed like products of it. They could no longer accept being ordinary humans because of their beliefs that they were something more. If you refused to feed their egos, they would swear a world of pain to be visited upon you.

They immediately became attached to me and my gift, desperately trying to make it their own, promising to be the dominating force in my short life. They think and behave immaturely, wanting to respond with brutality every time I said no. Having psychic ability surely leaves scars when surrounded by people like this.

They spoke of wanting my bloodline as part of theirs, living my life, and raising my children while I would be put in a mental home. He would salivate at the sound of his own words when talking of "wrestling those kids away" from me and making "him one of us." They wanted to frame me, imprison me, scar my face, and blind my eye. He spoke of wanting to "lock me in a dungeon and feed me the newspaper." They swore biological warfare and the weaponization of disease and infection— pursuing every avenue of revenge like true career cultists and satanic ritual abusers.

They promised to make me poor and homeless, saying I would never work in "their" town. He called himself "God around here" and said I would be persecuted and tormented everywhere I went—even if I ordered food in a random shop, it would be spat in. He swore "we don't take no for an answer" and that if I refused, they would find another way to take what they asked for. He suggested that he could give me a disability, and spoke of his desire to become a Baphomet. He promised to transform me into a "brain in a jar" for their own personal use—using my mind and spirit for their benefit while limiting the risk of me interrupting their plans or raising any alarm.

I was told I would be boycotted, isolated, kidnapped, tortured, and killed in a blood sacrifice—cut up alive and never found. I was already dead; they just needed to "figure out what to do with the body."

But I was also their ticket to Elysium and permanence of power. I was their dream come true, if only I was willing to grant their wishes. They could use me to buy support and bribe their supporters into helping them tell lies on a much larger scale. They could be rich and powerful, controlling society for generations with the information I could provide. They suggested that conspiracies only work when you get everyone involved. They seemed to believe that they could rewrite history, crown themselves holy and royal, messianic and worthy, and convince the world of their superiority and favor in the eyes of God.

As these distant memories replayed intensely in my mind, I felt broken, powerless, helpless, alone, afraid, confused, and unsure if I could ever prove a single fact or escape this feigned obscurity.

They called themselves Republicans, fighting for "freedom" and "the cause," but I only saw their selfish quest to become rich and royal through their far-fetched ego trip. I suspected they were working with the very forces they pretended to fight against—in the true vein of psychological warfare. It seemed as though forces from both sides had staged a coup of the early revolution, forcibly taking control of a legitimate campaign for rights and equality, and transforming it into a criminal crusade for wealth, power, and authority.

The protest for equality became a quest for privilege. The peaceful method became violent, managed and protected by corruption. They blamed soldiers and foreign intelligence networks for conspiring against us while mirroring that system and called it fair. They claimed to mourn thirteen civilians but killed so many more. They labelled us traitors for challenging the narrative or questioning the cost. They swore they were only at war with the Queen while waging a sadistic war of vengeance against anyone who opposed them. There truly was no straight path when dealing with these crooks.

They had stolen everything of value in this country—and sometimes destroyed it during the raid. Every item of worth was under siege. When caught and imprisoned, they planted bombs, held the nation hostage with threats of more, and then were all set free.

Thirty years of criminal warfare and a cross-national campaign of terrorism. Many innocents were knowingly framed by the British authorities, almost as if they were purposely avoiding having to catch the ones who were truly responsible. Another convincing reason for the true believers in the cause of violence against violence and authoritative abuses. I felt that we had all been truly fooled. Led on down the winding path that never goes home, never back to the start, but somewhere new, filled with more carnage and disguise. As though we can no longer recognise its true purpose, hidden under the cover of chaos, trauma, and destruction. Yet another distraction, a finger of blame, and more pandemonium, so we may have to deny the plentiful truths that, by now, would surely make us all look guilty.

THE PAINFUL JOURNEY

Becoming Aware

Almost as soon as I finished school and began working, I started to hear voices. The first time I heard them, I was working in a Georgian Palladian mansion that was built around 1770. It was being restored for private ownership, public visits, and a window into our checkered history. There was a very deep history associated with this parcel of land and the many structures that stood upon it. It was previously the residence of the Protestant Church of Ireland's regional Lord Bishop. The site had also been the Catholic Bishops' residence in the diocese for over one thousand years. This place was even a focus of pagan Druid worship in more ancient times, until the local people are said to have been converted by Saint Brecan in

570 AD, followed by the building of a Christian church by Saint Ultan (first Regional Catholic Bishop) sometime in the 600s. I remember the lads on site saying that it was once raided in 900 AD, and around 900 workers were locked into the buildings which were then set ablaze. This turned out to be partly true.

In 1031, the Abbey was raided and burned by the Danes of Dublin, with 200 people being killed in the fires and 200 more taken as captives. At that time, it was already a Christian settlement with churches and monasteries. Between 900 and 1150, it was the target of many raids by numerous clans and tribes, including Vikings, the O'Brien clan (descendants of the Munster King Brian Boru), and even the infamous Diarmuid MacMurrough—the deposed High King who travelled to England's King Henry II around 1166.

He allied with the English Normans to forcefully take back the throne of Leinster, effectively ending the significance of Ireland's High Kingship by passing the title to a Norman. This act signaled the end for the ancient system of domestic governance that had dominated this island for thousands of years.

I suppose, thinking of it now, it was a strange place for my hallucinations to begin—a site of pagan worship, brutal massacres of peaceful villagers, plus many age-old battles and raids. This place was a valued piece of land in a rich agricultural county, eventually seized as a symbol of power by a foreign occupation, where they would build an oversized mansion to dominate the region and intimidate its people. The natives lived in squalor and worked the land just to live, while the installed lordship classes lived in luxury as kings of a foreign territory. I did not know all of that at the time, and I never really connected it to my hallucinations until over a decade later.

I had only worked there for a couple of months but it was probably in the first couple of weeks when the subtle conversations from outside began. When I was inside, the voices would mostly seem to be coming from outside, with the sounds apparently coming through the windows, but emanating from somewhere among the trees or the wide-open fields just beyond the fence. After a couple of days of noticing the mumble-like noises, and as it got louder and clearer, I began to recognize some voices as people I knew. They were friendly at first, pretending they followed me to work to play a silly joke, but that was just to lull me into listening, or so I would be curious enough to allow them continue talking.

Sometimes, if I was deeper inside the building, the voices would be coming from the ceiling in the corner of the room. It was such a strange experience, and I was very confused as to how this was happening. At first, it was far away and muffled, like hearing a distant crowd filled with chatter and background noise where it's hard to focus on what any one voice might be saying, but after a while, it was as though they stopped talking to each other, and their attention became more focused on me.

As those first crowd-like noises continued, some of the individual voices were becoming more dominant than the others, and they were starting to lead the crowd of chatterers. Then they began to talk directly to me. It was mostly girls, and various girls that I had known throughout my years of growing up. The prominent voices were always female, but it seemed as though they were being directed by male voices that were not clearly audible. It was such a peculiar and alien experience, like I was hearing a book or script being read aloud by some very convincing voice actors, so extremely animated, using tone and emotion masterfully, slowly stealing my attention and drawing me in, never knowing what they would say next.

It began to get very personal, and the discussion became constantly centred on me. They then began pretending to read my mind but getting me very wrong; they were playing very clever and distracting mind games with me, attempting to provoke me into responding aggressively. As soon as it became obvious that they were directing all of their attention toward me I then began to hear them at night as I tried to sleep. In the calm of night they would seem louder as there were no environmental distractions or background noises. They would deliberately try to keep me awake by stressing me out and forcing me into reacting emotionally with anger and resentment, but keeping it all inside. The more angry, distressed, and sleep-deprived I became, the louder they would get. When it got to the stage where I was waking up distressed and emotionally charged, which happened quite quickly, they would begin to talk first thing in the morning, sometimes from before I could even open my eyes, and as soon as that happened, they would be talking three or four at a time, all day, every day, for at least six years.

It had gotten louder and more prominent until there were so many voices saying so many different things, sometimes talking all at once, sometimes singing childishly, sometimes there were whispers while one spoke for the group, they even shouted and screamed and tried to confuse me or hurt my feelings and exasperate me for ignoring them. They would even talk like an a cappella group, repeating the same sentence in four different voices, slightly out of sync, and then repeating a second sentence, then a third, and so on and so forth. It became absolutely excruciating and unbearable. I could not concentrate on anything, and even when conversing with a real person, I could not focus on their voice or absorb what they were saying at all. They made everything, even simple tasks, utterly impossible.

If I was working with loud machines, I would hear thirty or more voices screaming so loud that it would hurt my ears. Cement mixers, drills, Kango hammers, whackers, sanding machines, even household appliances like hoovers or hairdryers—they would scream from the second it was turned on until the second it was switched off, to the point that even though they were still talking, switching off the noisy machines still felt like some form of peace or relief. They would scream louder than the machinery, so loud that my brain felt like it was vibrating from the resonance of the sound waves.

I was under a constant barrage of screams and whispers, and a continuous conversation about me, which I played no part in. One time, I woke up suddenly during the night, sat up with my hands covering my ears because of what sounded like white noise or radio static at max volume. It took me a few seconds to decipher the multiples of different sounds, and then I realized it was just a very large group of simultaneous voices, possibly every single voice I had ever heard or that was ever familiar to me, all talking and shouting at once. Over the next few minutes, they calmed down and began to talk more normally, explaining that they were going to keep talking and harassing me until I answered them, even though they never actually asked any genuine questions, just smart remarks and sarcastic comments. I was a complete prisoner, and under an absolute siege.

There were times when the voices would seem to sneak up behind me and breathe heavily on the back of my neck, or whisper near my ear, and sometimes even seeming to brush past me. If I was walking down the street, they would move around from one side of the street to the other, really simulating the experience of being followed by more than one group of actual people, who had to move when I moved. There did always seem to be a line of sight between me and where the voices seemed to be coming from, although it was always a corner, or tree or a wall, or somewhere real people might manage be to stay out of sight.

They would often distract me, making me clumsy, causing me to break things, cups, glasses, anything at all. And when it happened, they would laugh and sneer and call me stupid, giving themselves so much credit for being intelligent enough to sabotage me. They rejoiced when they hurt me, and always seemed to be trying to catch me out or trip me up or confuse me when I was trying to concentrate on anything else.

Even reading was literally painful; the voices would shout aloud every word I read, and if I read too fast, they would be trailing after, and sometimes even spoke in an echo-like pattern where there might be four or five different voices clamoring the words as I read them, each voice one or two words behind the other. If I kept reading, it would just start to sound like a crowd babbling, or multiple radio stations clashing in the air around me. I had zero control over them, and they would make a point of trying to destroy any attempt by me to turn my attention to anything other than them. Every single thing I did was a battle, and one that they would always try to win!

Another time, I was at home in the family house where I lived when, suddenly, I heard extremely loud music. It was so loud that the walls of the house seemed to be vibrating, but the music was not coming from outside, even though it was like being near an open-air concert. It was like opera music, but much more modern and eclectic. I could hear the singing voices of Bono and Andrea Corr, and what resembled an ambient-style orchestral or instrumental piece. It sounded very organized and synchronized, a beautiful symphony that was actually quite relaxing and peaceful. A song that no human had ever heard—or ever will again! I was quite confused and never spoke of it until years later, but thinking of it now, I actually feel kind of privileged. I know that most people would be afraid and could never relate to or understand an experience like that, but I had learned to live with those seemingly alien occurrences, as they had plagued my mind and life, day and night for over a decade. They would not let me sleep or relax or allow me to feel calm or confident so an experience like mysterious music was as much of a relief as it was frightening or confusing.

I suppose by around the age of 24, when I started driving, and I found other things to do with my mind that did not require too much concentration, they had become much less conspicuous and demanding. Game consoles or Pitch and Putt or snooker had helped me to focus, without having to try too hard to use words or commands to encourage my own mind. Those kinds of activities required just enough brainpower to distract me without alerting them. The uninterrupted and unending conversation had mostly faded out by then, although not completely. There did seem to be a balance involved when dealing with "them." If I was doing physical work and my mind was idle, they were loud. If I was concentrating too hard, they would abuse and distract me, repeating and amplifying my every thought, and often shouting random comments to break my train of thought. But there did seem to be a "goldilocks zone" where they might fall silent, even if it was only for a moment. Although, as soon as you might realize they had become quiet, they would let you know that they were still "there." I guess the lull periods became increasingly extended until they had finally disappeared completely.

Crowds and commotion were still quite mentally challenging, but that tended to be a familiar consequence of my experience of auditory hallucinations, i.e., that the vibration and reverberation of noisy, bustling spaces were identical to my experience of being vocally vociferated in perpetuity. So, even without continual hallucinations, crowded locations would be a likely trigger, even though these bouts of "voices" were no longer permanent and constant. I had developed quite bad anxiety when in busy public spaces due to the voices always attempting to humiliate and embarrass me by screaming obscenities or suggesting that I do cruel or violent things to weaker members of the crowd. As much as I hated them constantly trying to force a negative reaction out of me, there were also times when they did make me laugh, probably not because they were funny, but most of what they might tend to say was almost always unexpected. But I had, for the first time in my adult life, found at least some moments of peace.

It's A Slow Process

The human brain is clearly an incredibly fascinating and powerful organic machine. I had no idea that it could simulate those kinds of experiences for its host. I guess for a long time I felt like it was attacking me, but now I feel more like it was trying to tell me something that my conscious mind had been forced to forget, similar to post-traumatic stress disorder or a delayed fight-or-flight response. It probably triggered during hypnosis all those years ago. During early development, my mind was vandalized and as my brain matured, it was out of sync with my personality, unable to become fully aware and independently in control of all the things that happened to me when I was put into a hypnotic trance. It is a difficult situation to describe, like becoming more aware when you are hypnotized, but then unaware that you were hypnotized.

Your eyes are closed, and you are in total darkness, while being in a very large room with maybe twenty or thirty different people, all strangers, and probably all aware that you are in a purposely induced trance. They were all interacting with each other, leaving you frozen and alone, and using all your other senses to figure it all out. I guess that could make your secondary senses hypersensitive and hyperaware, only without the knowledge of your own conscious mind.

From the moment those hallucinations became loud and clear, I knew there was something I was missing. I know that they spoke the way they did because they wanted me to listen to them, and I also knew that the more attention you give them, the more they will lead you on into verbal abuse and manipulation to a regrettable end. They had made it clear that I could never trust them, but they also claimed to be helping me and training my mind, while insinuating that everyone else was out to get me.

But they were constantly dropping hints or phrasing their suggestive comments to spark suspicion, intrigue, and curiosity. They were consistently trying to get you to think or ask, "What do you mean by that?" or "Why would you say that?" and "Do you know something that I don't?". There was a blindingly obvious truth that they knew something that I did not, or maybe they just wanted me to think that. Either way, that was something I would have to figure out by myself, for myself, and in a way that did not involve them but was rooted in the shared reality of the real and physical world.

NO LONGER A CHILD

The Moment Of Truth

Sunday 19th November 2011, 2:30 AM

Being induced into another trance at the age of twenty-nine triggered a great many revelations for me:

• Repressed memories—the missing pieces of my disordered mind.

• Hypnosis had been weaponised against me from a young age, leaving me vulnerable to manipulation and social abuses.

• The realisation that I could tell the future.

• Facing the truth that I am the present incarnation of an unimaginably powerful gift that has been carried by some of the most influential and mysterious characters in all of world history.

• Knowing that people around me not only knew but had conspired against me and helped to orchestrate and conceal some of the most traumatic incidents of my life.

• I was surrounded by gangs and private armies that had an agenda and were intent on punishing me for not aligning with them.

• Seemingly petty criminals were using the same advanced information-extraction tactics as world-class spies and interrogators, e.g. Guantanamo Bay Detention Camp.

• I was consistently limited in maturing economically and socially— deliberately stunted in virtually all aspects of personal development since a very young age.

• My family had basically loaned me out, as a child, to the local gangster/terrorist.

• Forces within the government and civil service were aiding in a criminal conspiracy against me.

• The "mafia" wanted my bloodline and legacy to divide among their clans and aimed to control the prophetic gift for generations to come.

• Some of those around me had aided in committing an international crime that triggered a brutal and illegal war, economic chaos, financial meltdown, and unprecedented levels of global debt.

• They were being directed by international elements.

• All of this was being orchestrated by the most powerful players in the global political, military, and financial hierarchy.

All of this knowledge rushed back into my mind but disappeared again when I was awakened from my trance. It slowly came back to me again over the next couple of months, like a ton of bricks, crashing into me a thousand times a day, every day, for 5 years. I was brainwashed while hypnotised, and made to talk constantly, verbally describing my every single thought as they came to me. This kind of interrogation tactic is a lot like being under perpetual supervision and cross-examination, resulting in me talking to myself as those memories were leaking back into my brain on slow-release, causing mania, insomnia, restlessness, internalised aggression, high stress, and an inability to wind down or slow my mind. I was grappling with my own mind as I tried to trigger the memories of those lost events that shaped my whole world and influenced everyone around me. These forgotten experiences and traumatic memories, some over two decades old, were playing on a loop in my brain, escalating my emotional state to uncontrollable levels of anger and resentment, fear and suspicion, and feeling trapped with my abusers and their enablers, dooming me to be maltreated by my captors who had stolen and traded parts of my life, and knowledge, and shared it amongst themselves.

The Truth Hurts

I was starting to feel a lot like a fully grown Satan—the boy who destroyed the world, wreaking havoc and spreading chaos, sharing dangerous knowledge with the cruel, evil, and brutally ambitious. I had truly lost my mind.

I was isolated and avoiding people I would normally spend most of my time with. I became trapped with my own amplified thoughts and soul-destroying memories. My own personal life, its repetitive routine, and especially my overloaded mind started to feel very much like a crowded and chaotic prison. There was no escaping or leaving any of it behind. I had absolutely no coping mechanism for situations such as these; they were so far outside of myself and any kind of control. I had no true friends, no allies, no plan, no one to talk to, and no end to the madness.

The utter chaos that had erupted in the Middle East had now spread to Syria. The people were fleeing, and I was reading the news every day, crying uncontrollably. Those brutal and savage events were still very much in motion, and I could not cope with any part of it. I had no idea where to begin. I was convinced that I would be ignored, killed, or institutionalised if I tried to tell my truth. I did not care so much when I thought I was dealing with my own problems, but feeling the weight and responsibility for circumstances that were this destructive was not something any normal person could ever be prepared to remedy or react to. I felt hopeless and, well, insane, to be honest. I was alone in this struggle and helpless in this far-fetched nightmare. I guess I knew that there must be a path forward for us all. I may not know what it is yet, but I will not give in. I will be the devil to beat the devil, if I have to!

It's a Dark Gift - But I See the Light

It is difficult to describe what this gift is or what it feels like when I use it. It feels like a darkness inside that I can see when I am under hypnotic trance, but instead of seeing or knowing myself, I become only aware of others. It's almost like I don't exist anymore—only the world does. This darkness carries me far, pushing me forward through time, accelerating me so fast that light just passes through me as I pass it right by. It is like being surrounded by darkness but sensing the light so very far away. It was as if I could will myself forward to investigate that light and absorb the information it contained.

At first, I had control; I could see myself in the future, almost communicating telepathically with him, and he was starting to remember and understand. I could read what he was reading and I called out every word aloud. I could somehow encourage him to seek out information we were both curious about. It was then like drawing it backward through time, toward myself. It was blowing my mind up—in all different directions, all at the same time.

But then I started to realise that I did not have control. This dark gift was controlling me, and when I wanted to stop or slow down, it kept dragging me forward, unable to let me go. I wanted to wake up, but they wouldn't let me. I wanted to be human, but it had turned me into something else—almost like I had become some kind of four-dimensional object simultaneously occupying multiple locations in space-time. Or I was now part of a group of particles entangled by an invisible quantum link, all receiving information from the future and transmitting it far back into the past. No language barriers exist in this place, like we (the line of prophets) can be all different people sharing the same mind, or occupying the same multi-dimensional space, like the mythical Tower of Babel that reaches up to the heavens and speaks the master tongue, the language of God.

At one stage, while I was in a trance, it was like I had ascended into the heavens and saw the Earth from space. I could see an arched column of holographic screens laid out in front of me. I could imagine each one as a different time in my future life or the universe at a different age or future location in time. I could picture travelling along that curved road as it stretched toward infinity, choosing exactly when I wanted to go next. But my imagination ran wild, and it became difficult to separate the true reality of my ability from the visual representation I had created in my mind. I guess I began to understand how some people could break away from reality because of hypnosis or believe themselves to be actual gods. But I wanted to wake up; they did not!

The Difficult Road Is The Righteous Path

I guess I had to accept the worst parts of myself and the obvious flaws of one man or child carrying such ultimate power with no real control over its limits. A gift like that would drive you mad, as would the people who lust after it. But that same curse/gift, and my fellow companions who carried it, should also be the way out of this labyrinth of dead ends that I found myself faced with, in whatever direction I tried to go.

I read his words and summarised his many known lifetimes, and I started to feel more at peace—more in alignment and harmony with his intentions. Even if I could not fully remember the future I saw, I could still look for guidance from those who did, the men who saw further than me and were surrounded by much better companions and apostles, some of whom had altruistic designs for the people of our time. They spoke in riddles and gave us cryptic clues, but they chose someone who would tell the truth— identified by fate and world events, someone they could trust, someone they believed in, someone they knew, someone who is just like them.

The ones who wrote the books and authored the true prophecies, indicating the right time to reveal their encoded secrets, surely left directions for the one to whom it all falls down upon. Zarathustra, Daniel, Muhammad, and Nostradamus are just some who had spoken of these times and the rampant corruption and greed that would ensnare the world. I see men with no real skills or new knowledge, but people trained to gamble and speculate and take advantage of their place in the world—manipulating the economy to increase their share or inflate their stock, not really adding any value to the economy for most people, but moving their bets around to swell their own pockets. Siphoning wealth away from the working classes and devaluing the currency as if money has completely lost its meaning to them. It is a mere tool, a weapon, or a cloak and dagger to betray the masses who depend on a fair and just system—the system that promises to raise up the best in society so that they can improve the apparatus for everyone else, but that is not the function it fulfils.

Nations are trillions in debt—realistically unpayable sums—and politics are scripted and treated as theatre. They use their privilege to share knowledge of the system with their allies and supporters, creating an entire class of gamblers and speculators, getting rich by ignoring the exploitation of its flaws and carrying on as if nothing had changed. Every time they launch a rocket, trigger a war, threaten tariffs, or award contracts, every time the markets fluctuate, they are winning, and they are gaming the system. All while the banks win, and win, and win again.

Self-Proclaimed Holy Warriors and the Madness of Kings

The situation in Gaza is unbearably cruel. I never would have thought that I would witness someone reading from the Bible like it was Mein Kampf— until I saw Binyamin Netanyahu quoting Amalek. One of the most frightening things I have ever seen on live television, only comparable to George Bush telling the world, "Either you are with us, or you are with the terrorists." Two of the most dangerous people that the world has ever known. They have destroyed nations together, even their own! What worries me is what's backing them up, pulling their strings, or, even worse, placing them into power in the first place.

There is very obviously an agenda at play for men like that to break so many laws and still get the red carpet and rounds of applause. To indirectly threaten half the world's governments, peoples, and economies. To commit genocide while claiming to be preventing one. Arming and training terrorists, and blaming religion for their actions. Every dirty trick is an obvious lie, and every lie is an admission of truth.

My Purpose

I am not sure how to proceed. My mind was broken, my life was corrupted, and my many possible paths in life have been all but blocked. I have so much information inside, but I can't be sure who to share it with. I also have to be mindful that the worst possible candidates already know the future of the world and humanity. If the world is unbalanced, maybe I should share the future with their rivals, hopefully taking away any advantage that deceitful elements have managed to seize for their own.

This journey has been long for him, and I sense that he wants to find some peace and encourage true balance. I often feel the deepest sense that he has been locked in a dungeon for thousands of years, fed lies and punished for still knowing the truth. He has been used to keep the same people in power for millennia and the only reason they did not conquer the world sooner was the power struggle that raged on between themselves.

I used to feel like the world was ending and that it was all somehow my fault—that I had failed the task that God gave to him, or that maybe I was just the number, and the omen that signals the end. I felt like the whole world was staging a play, leading me on and dishonestly pretending that I don't exist or that I am unimportant, unwanted, and powerless. But I also know that his words echoed throughout the ages and found me, repairing my traumatised and broken mind and reconnecting me to our immortal spirit.

No matter the task or my place in the line, I must help others find truth and peace, accepting our collective purpose.

I hope that we are still young as a species and that our global society can become more about survival and unity than money and power.

He has changed. The Earth has changed. We must also adjust and reconfigure our ideals and our values. We must invest in the environment. It is our greatest asset.

I would be lying if I said that I am not afraid. He will always be outgunned and outnumbered, and in possession of something that everyone else wants to have. I don't expect to be wanted or accepted, and I definitely do not think that I can talk everyone down or lull them into compliance or compromise. I know that I cannot replace the best versions of him, but this is what fate or God or Heaven has made me, and I could not change it if I tried. I have to accept it, whether I want this gift or not.

I am glad that we finally live in a world where everyone can understand my explanations about our origins and the supernatural abilities that have passed down along our evolutionary path. I could never claim to fully understand exactly what this is, and in some ways, I think that the ancient man he used to be had to see this far just to better understand those things about himself. So, I may not be the best of him, but we do have at least some of the knowledge he was seeking. I hope that everyone can know his story as our story and believe in his purpose as our purpose. And I truly hope that we can make the best of it, instead of childishly fighting over details that no one will ever get to pick.

THE AUTHORITY OF GOD

God Told Me

As soon as I knew who I was and what it meant, I felt that I should focus all my energy on aiding Palestine in what must seem like their eternal quest for freedom, sovereignty, and self-determination. One Holocaust does not justify another, and it seems that Israel is taking every advantage and demanding special treatment as a nation because of the brutal Nazi genocide.

In its early stages, Nazism and Zionism were aligned in their quest to exile European Hebrews to Palestine. The "Third Reich" even facilitated the transfer of Jewish wealth from Germany to the new political settlements in British Mandate Palestine. Various Zionist militias took part in a campaign of terrorism, kidnapping, bombings, and massacres, even while European Hebrews were being hunted and placed into "work" camps.

While Nazism targeted European Hebrews, Zionism pushed forward in its pursuit of conquering the holy lands of their ancient ancestors. This secondary campaign of violence, dispossession, and extermination against the Hebrew family tree still rages on over 80 years later. While Nazism has been acknowledged as a great crime, Zionism has been afforded a status of exceptionalism and awarded limitless amounts of Western funding and artillery, described as "aid." The global media conglomerate provides cover for the crimes of the Western-backed colony and manufactures support—or the illusion of support—throughout the global north.

The new age Evangelical Christianity that arose in North America has become Zionism's most dedicated following. Their pastors and preachers regularly convince congregations that it is their "duty" to pledge unquestioning allegiance to the modern state of Israel, with some even directly stating that "God has commanded it." These are the kinds of psychological warfare tactics used by medieval popes and kings. Modern Israeli politicians and Zionist rabbis also employ this strategy to attract support from within the Jewish diaspora and evade accountability for their illegal, unjust, and extremist actions. They regularly claim that the world wants to exterminate Israel, or that their "enemies" want to commit a second Holocaust.

Their Messiah has been missing for thousands of years, although historians question whether he ever even existed at all. The Torah was most likely written by men who were council to the prophets— their holy men of God (who have also been A.W.O.L since ancient times). Even Rome has ruled for nearly two thousand years in the place of a man whom they brutally tortured and executed. These facts have given the ruling and moneyed classes a huge number of liberties in their approach to God, his commands, his chosen representative, and his instructions for a just world.

During colonisation and slavery, the same strategy was used against foreign peoples. Soldiers were blessed and "forgiven," both before and after participating in brutal mass murders and forced conversions of the "soulless beasts" and "barbarians." History tells us that we have been lied to and misled many times over by those who were merely seeking wealth, power, and more followers to aid in conquering lands, controlling resources, and collecting taxes.

Personally, I do not think that God gives clear instructions in human language. It seems to me that God is too powerful and alien to directly communicate with any human being. This would explain why he sends his angels as envoys, or anoints an honest and true prophet. I think there is logic, science, and rules involved in God's instructions, but they tend to come from the natural world and the threats that we face, and they are usually things that we must figure out for ourselves, together.

There does seem to be a kind of cloud involved when he uses the gift—not a white or bright cloud, but more like a dark, black space which appears to be empty but is actually compacted with cosmic information. I think that when those rules, logic, or instructions are communicated through a prophet, they come from a place beyond human explanation, probably the result of many different logical equations based on current and future knowledge or fact, converging around this temporary nexus who can decipher some of the things that we do not understand and cannot see. I have been to this place, and I do trust that God—and the one who carries his gift—always must have the best intentions for the world and everyone in it.

The Banks Always Win

Nazism wiped out all significant naturalised political and social resistance to Zionism from within the extensive Jewish community. They created the conditions for the legitimised political pivot in the West toward unchecked Zionism, supporting it at all costs, and convincing the electorate that it is our moral duty to reinforce and condone the actions of extreme Zionism.

The Nazi campaign against European Jewry also became the reason that debate and discussion which was not in full support of Zionism effectively became illegal and punishable by law, equating it with the endorsement of antisemitism and support of Nazism.

The Continuation of Many Empires

Eighty years later, laws are still being drafted to curtail any legitimate social movement in favour of Palestine's natural rights and legitimate claim to nationhood and independence. The West is becoming ever more draconian and authoritarian when it comes to its own citizenry protesting the extreme violence and self-interest of the Israeli state or expressing doubt surrounding the maximum bias of the entire narrative.

Israel is a unique state that is afforded a status of exception when it commits international crimes of war and other heinous acts. We in the West are fed a repetitive mantra about defence rights rather than analysing and challenging the legality of their behaviour, while completely sidestepping the obvious facts of Palestinian rights and legal claims under a fair and equal system of laws. We are also shamed and bullied into accepting the fantasy of Israel's manufactured image of sainthood and purity, constantly sold the idea that if we don't excuse their aggression, we will be partaking in or responsible for another Holocaust.

The Zionist state of Israel is an extremist and racist project that deliberately attracts some very violent elements to join its ranks and partake in its abuses. People are indoctrinated and encouraged to commit acts of barbarity against the natives of Palestine, while under government or tribal protection and without fear of prosecution or retribution. They rewrote the laws of the land to favour themselves and enforce martial law across all the territories that the Palestinians have been confined to.

Israel is the only nation on Earth that can pick and choose its citizens based on their political affiliations. They import extremists and supporters, granting them citizenship, while barring renowned Jewish leftists from even visiting the nation. The Israeli government seems to have the unique ability of importing voters that will reinforce their ideology and militaristic aspirations bringing the country even further into extremism, racism, and the rejection of Palestinian rights to freedom, equality, justice, and prosperity.

Aggressive Response

The modern Zionist project has adopted and modified all the old-world strategies of British imperial colonisation, the American campaign against its natives, and even the Nazi-style laws that were drafted to scapegoat German Jews. All logical and obvious conclusions are turned on their heads when dealing with the Israeli narrative. The politicians of Israel and their biggest supporters talk as if they are either severely indoctrinated into aggressively forcing their perspective on others, or even brainwashed into being unable to accept an opposing or more inclusive view. It might also be self-evident to conclude that they are extensively trained in psychological warfare strategies when engaging with moderates so as to take control of the discussion, redirect attention and blame, and force others into shame, frustration, and silence. Manipulators and abusers always employ conversational tactics such as these to convince their victims and opponents that they are wrong, paranoid, mistaken, or confused. These types of strategies are highly effective in many situations of coercive control with the aim of making your target dependent on you, suspicious or unsure of everyone else, or guilty enough to blame themselves—allowing themselves to be punished, and even encouraging others to attack and blame them for you.

Zionism has virtually unlimited funds and incredible political might which has an iron grip on the politics and economics of many Western nations. They virtually behave as one nation or system of governments, no matter what their respective citizens think or want. Protests, marches, and legal challenges—the only reaction of governments is to try and outlaw their cause, equating it with terrorism, genocide, and neo-Nazism. Protesters have been prosecuted, deported, accused of racism, demonetised, banned from social platforms, fired, blacklisted, raided, arrested by immigration services, and even had their college degrees revoked or withheld. Ordinary people are risking their jobs and careers for expressing their "political" views. Even moderate social media posts can now be grounds to revoke visas and have you detained, interrogated, and refused entry—all in the "liberal and free" West.

This dystopian world is again to benefit the wealthy Western cabal (who all appear to have descended from medieval European royalty), as they shift away from democratic values and resist democratic change. Money has unashamedly poisoned the political process and given us brutally limited options. The American system, most of all, has always resisted change, coming down hard on many widespread cultural movements domestically. They have assassinated leaders and destroyed many foreign governments that aligned with socialism and rejected the Western economic and financial system.

The Snowball Effect

A nameless empire has been crawling across the earth since civilisation began: Sumer to Egypt, Jerusalem to Rome, London to Washington, and back to Jerusalem. But just as Britain, once a Roman colony, became more brutal, ruthless and greater than its father, America had also conquered its mother. And now Israel seems to dominate them both, even though it's only a fraction of their size. Israel seems to completely control almost the entire (but narrow) political spectrum in the States. It's almost beyond comprehension how much influence it has or how much money it spends deciding both the contestants and the outcome of almost every election. The lobby groups are entirely shaping politics in numerous nations. Even in Britain, the newspapers attack and smear political opponents of Zionism. It's absolutely unbelievable how much Israel's interests close down debate and discussion and narrow the political spectrum to such a degree that there is virtually ZERO difference between the opposition and the ruling party, where election candidates of opposing parties are almost carbon copies of each other. I am completely dumbfounded. Where is the choice?

Moneyed interests have utterly destroyed politics and stifled debate; people have almost no influence at all over policy. Politics has become stale and only serves the needs of the banks, the military complex, and the megacorporations. Every single election cycle, they gain more power, more wealth, fewer taxes, fewer regulations, and even more influence over all of these authorities. Freedoms are being eroded. Nations are becoming powerless. Capitalism has become communism; only states don't exist, merely economic zones administered by the banks. It is a form of fascism, with only the illusion of choice—but that illusion is becoming less and less convincing. One party, one goal, one class, one bank, and to very large degree, one race. No one can defeat the beast that it has become!

THE HUMAN OMNIPRESENCE

Ghosts Can't Read The Newspaper

One of the reasons that I believe he is always among us is that the prophets of old have given us so much detail about the world and the times that we live in. They could not have known such specifics without experiencing and seeing it for themselves. They described machines, technology, phone numbers, dates, locations, and names. I do believe that those gifts of knowledge do come from God, but I do not believe that God "told" them.

God, to me, seems more like the fabric of the universe or an energy field that is in constant flux, never still or static but an immensely powerful motion that is somehow dense and heavy but still fluid, viscous, massless, and fast-moving. At times, it can be difficult to hold onto the information this gift can acquire because this black sea of energy that you find yourself in is ever-changing and rapid, and there is no reverse flow or going backward; it is a ceaseless force that can only push forward.

Merkaba

At one point, it seemed as though I was inside a layered glass sphere, similar to Russian dolls, where each layer could move independently, aligning to express different coordinates—like a true star gate, providing a window to different times and locations. That's not really an accurate representation of how the gift works in practice, but after what felt like an eternity for my mind, I was starting to feel like I was trapped inside a black hole, and as the universe was changing and aging around me, somehow, I remained the same.

A Pagan King

At another stage during my entranced experience I saw a primitive man dancing around a bonfire. He looked quite dirty and was barely dressed, wearing mostly dried vegetation like grasses and leaves. He seemed to be taking part in a tribal festival or ritual as he wore an animal's skull on his head that was probably placed there by his own clan. It was a very large skull that completely covered his head, with the jaws resting upon his shoulders. It had very large horns and seemed to have been dried to the point where it's skin had become red leather. It looked very like a bulls skeletal cranium except it had straw or dried grasses between it's horns that resembled hair. I kind of laughed a little as I watched this strange yet vivid scene. Suddenly the young man stopped dancing and bowed his head or maybe nodded—as if listening intently or had simply heard my spontaneous reaction and was acknowledging his awareness of me. This kind of frightened me as it was extremely unexpected and the scene I was observing abruptly disappeared.

I was taken aback both when this imagery became so clear to me that it was like seeing it with my eyes, but I was especially startled when the man appeared to become aware of me watching. I was left with this idea of a pagan king, but it also suddenly seemed as though I was the man in the vision. I became rather uncomfortable as I immediately felt like I was the one wearing the horned skull with straw hair, right now, in the present. I instantaneously felt like I saw myself as a pagan king in the modern world who had been crowned by the ancients, and it is a very difficult idea to process or understand. It was so unexpected and incredibly strange but also eerily accurate and impossible to accept.

He Is What It Is

I have been aware of what I carry for almost fourteen years. It has been such a struggle to accept it without logical thinking, concerning the accepted parameters of normal life experience, telling me that I have lost my mind. Even knowing that I have the gift or believing that I will be the one to fulfil the coming prophecies are, very obviously, two completely different things. Many have had the gift, but we only know a few of their names, almost as if one is enough to install a government and create a ruling class, but everyone they can find after that is treated like a prisoner, and their gift is used to enrich and empower the highest levels of society. I mourn for the nameless versions of him that were lost to history, and imprisoned or executed to instill fear among his loyal and true believers, and even the future versions of himself. Many others have suffered in his name or paid the price for believing in him. We have been trapped in the dark ages for the longest time. I certainly feel that I have.

I understand that there is only one, and the fact that he manifests in different tribes but still descends from the same ancestral line makes it moderately difficult for the empire to permanently possess him. He may habitually come from a neighbouring tribe, so no matter how much they move around, it must surely have been tricky to keep up. And even when they do find him, they would have to use more and more people just to take advantage of him.

It is a very strange idea that they call him the king of the world or the leader of world religions, while everything so many have done was to prevent that recurrence. And even if he gets there and dies a king he will still, most likely, be reborn a slave, of sorts. It's hard to imagine the supposedly divine leader of this earthly realm being reborn as a baby, but I guess that's just how he loses his seat of power (if he ever truly had one), then becoming a victim and prisoner of that same system of authority he helped to create.

I don't really subscribe to that "divine king" definition of what I am, but seeing how corruption and abuse of power are becoming more and more dangerously destructive for a large proportion of the earth's people—and even toxic to the environment—it's not difficult to understand why a "true saint" or "righteous soul" needs to have at least some influence over the system. It is probably true that he has never ruled over a modern empire or yet inherited any previous seat of power and authority, and that also does make it easier for him to appear flawlessly pure, or wise beyond normal human capacity.

This fact might also suggest that he may not be so saintly and true, but if his gift was pure knowledge, logic, and a universal understanding (when he uses it), he could only arrive at a fair and just conclusion. And even if he did not fully understand the complex matrices of information that he is exposed, he would still comprehend the fact that he will be returned to this society that he helped to construct. So if he gets it wrong or tries to cheat, he will have to live with the consequences of that imprudence from the other side of the desk.

I would also tend to believe that, in the hypothetical idea he did turn into a villain or become any type of dictator, he would most certainly learn what it means to be on the other end of that boot. So, whether or not you believe in the idea of a "divine soul" sent to guide us, you can surely understand why he genuinely does try to be as invested as possible in that righteous aspect of his supposed purpose.

I cannot claim to be a saint, and I should not have to live like a monk all the time, forever. But I do believe in logic, maths, science, and truth, and God is all of those things. I am obviously not super intelligent or all glory and divine, but I do believe in his purpose, and there is a necessary function in the world that he can fulfil—to create knowledge banks, promote structure and stability, encourage order and balance, and to counter some of the biggest flaws in human nature—going too far and not knowing when it's time to slow down or stop, or attempting to dominate and possess everything we can imagine.

He can act as an integral part of the information we collect and share with each other. He can foresee our collective future and warn us of catastrophe and danger. Potentially, he can siphon valuable ideas and complex knowledge from a future dimension of time and help us to replicate the best ideas and most advanced methods, reverse-engineering technological miracles. But we would have to be willing to share ideas and enhance access to further education for the masses. The more we know, the more he could know. He could help us to learn, seeking out knowledge to discover the best path forward in an increasingly challenging world.

When I use this talent, it feels the most comfortable and positive when I sense progress, harmony, advanced knowledge, and broad human success. It can be traumatising and painfully difficult to bear when I sense violence or disaster and then feel responsible and burdened, needing to alleviate the damage in some way or prevent it if possible.

He will always be new to this and may never feel that he is truly worthy, but still, it is a constant learning curve (or wave). I pray that there will always be new information and new knowledge, or a more extensive interpretation of old knowledge. I am inclined to think that the more minds he can reach and receive, the better and more useful his gift will become.

The Burden of Daniel

I am not very knowledgeable in the ancient history of Jerusalem, but the story of the Prophet Daniel is incredibly fascinating and somehow deeply familiar. There are two conflicting accounts of his most infamous challenges. The first is that he was a priest and prophet in Jerusalem when King Nebuchadnezzar of Babylon attacked, ransacked the city, destroyed the Temple, kidnapped the Prophet, and forced thousands of Jews into captivity.

The other version insinuates that the clergymen imprisoned Daniel to extract all the information his gift could acquire, and that the King of Babylon heard of his plight and invaded to rescue him, bringing him back to his palace to live in luxury and to teach the King about the wisdom of God.

Personally, and given my own struggles with hostility and attempted mind control, I think the latter is much more plausible, especially when considering the fate of Jesus and the path that the priesthood has navigated—and I do quite like the idea of a broken and embattled man being rescued by strangers who followed his spirit, or an innocent prisoner rescued only to be treated as a king. Daniel never returned to Jerusalem after his release, it is suspected that he wandered toward Persia and that his fellowship of captives willingly settled in Iran, preserving their culture and his legacy to this day.

I would imagine that Daniel carried a huge amount of guilt for the events in Jerusalem and the destruction of the city and its temple—

probably blaming himself and his gift for the coming fate of Jesus, having told the priesthood everything that would happen and all that it was worth to the future of the empire.

The Story of Christ

I do believe that Jesus' life was the result of the convergence of many prophecies—Daniel and Zarathustra foresaw his predicament. To me, it definitely seems possible that even Rome was following ancient prophecy when they conquered Jerusalem, empowered the priesthood, and supported a puppet king.

They all knew who he was since long before he even existed. They knew who his mother would be and where he would be born; there was no escaping his fate. It is even said that the wise Magi (priests and followers of Zarathustra) found him and ordained him, probably following ancient Iranian prophecy. I would guess that Daniel had told the clergymen everything, willingly or not, and they planned his death and defected to mighty Rome, becoming a vital piece of the new and "everlasting" empire. The ancient knowledge and belief in this reincarnated prophetic ability was subsequently erased from the public mind and eventually lost to time.

We get taught a very basic and oversimplified story of Jesus. I do not believe that God "willed" him to die on the cross or that God "sacrificed" his only son for us. I do not think that he died for our sins; I think that we killed him because we are sinners.

If the rich and powerful priests and monarchs of the ancient world realised the potential advantage of a practically immortal man who could see far into the future, no wonder they killed him in the minds of the people. Nowadays, it's easy to see why they wanted it for themselves—you could get rich overnight with his ability; advanced knowledge of stock market trends, the results of every single lotto draw, cryptocurrency fluctuations, and sports event results. And with significant amounts of cash to invest and a string of good business decisions, you could become ultra-rich in a very short space of time, without actually inventing or creating anything original of your own.

But more importantly, and relevant to that time and the kings of the old empires, they could find out the result of every war, which empire conquers the world or lasts beyond collapse, which kings to side with and which allies to support, who can be trusted or who will be overthrown, which lands are rich and which people can be conquered or converted, which religion will be accepted or which would be lost—these were the most important questions an ancient dynasty and empire could hope to know—and every throne, every dynasty, wanted to be the eternal one, and most in those times were obsessed with ruling over the known map

I would imagine that by the time Jesus was preaching, he knew the whole story of his life and death. I would hope that he found people he could trust to share the knowledge with. I would hope they told him all that he needed to know, and that he chose to become a king in death. The Line of Prophets will forever bear his name, and the obvious deception of Rome and the ancient clergy.

I tend to think that it does become a little overbearing to be this thing and carry this gift, and there can only be one who holds it, for the sakes of us all. To be so different while trying to help everyone else understand why, I do understand how it can feel like pressure, and a hopeless struggle against a much greater force than any single human being.

You might not always be ready to admit it and fear that you might not have all the answers or verifiably understand the gift or its origins. And even if he did reach the knowledge and find the reasons, it would be out of its own time. No one else would have had the capacity or knowledge base to understand it. They may misinterpret the imagery and think that you are not like the God they could comprehend or relate to. And even if you simplified the ideas, it becomes set in stone, and you end up being labelled a heretic when returning to expand on those strange and incomplete ideas.

Maybe he needed to learn from us for a change, or for the world to find its own path. I can understand why he may have wanted or needed to disappear. It can also be rather unfair to be such a heavy influence on everyone else's minds. We are meant to develop and grow without constant coaching. Even for me to find out who or what I am, without the weight of a born title and the pressure of being the prime example, I still felt like I was supposed to be the new and improved version of the greatest of him. And that is far too much for anyone to be expected live up to, or surpass.

I am sure that he does fear us, especially when he cannot give us the answers that we might want to hear.

I would say, though, that it might only be now, in these times, that we can finally understand what he is, or why he exists, or how he came to those conclusions, considering all we know about history, biology, physics, religion, prophecy, and his imminent return. I do not believe that blind belief in the words of an ancient book is what God and religion should be; I think that he should be able to prove his uniqueness and his connection, scientifically, to us all.

Nostradamus and the Holy Mother

It is deeply fascinating to feel this strong sense of being directly connected to an ancient human who may be trying to communicate specifically to me. To think of him lost throughout time, isolated; his gift and his words are his only salvation and his only path to redemption and spiritual freedom. I sense that he has had some unbearable experiences, and the guilt must be devastating for the power that his gift has given to the wrong people or the catastrophic events that he could not prevent or undermine. I perceive that he has felt ambushed and trapped, abused and forgotten, killed and erased, while his knowledge and ability were awarded to the lawless and untrue.

I know that the verses can be vague and cryptic and very easily misinterpreted. Still, there is something so deep and soothing when I think that he may be trying to contact his distant avatar, with his companions safeguarding his immortal words, preserved forever like they were carved in stone or baked in clay, to tell us of the day when we will all find each other, through each other, using the books as a guide. We shall all be finally free and have the answers that we have long searched for.

I believe, like most, that his fate is tied to that of the world, and for him to be free, we must all be free—in our minds and spirits, as well as in the physical world.

It's strange how vivid the impression is when I contemplate that Nostradamus may have spoken of me and to me. He wrote some letters to accompany his books, mostly addressed to the King of France or his own son Caesar, in which he iterates the main objective of his books, and the motivation behind them. When I read these letters I was left with the notion he was suggesting the purpose for some of the quatrains was to provide a guide for Jesus Christ on his return to human society, but this interpretation is very vague and mostly suggestive.

Michel de Nostredame seems to be a highly intelligent man and incredibly knowledgeable for a man of his time. I needed AI and information search engines just to understand the meaning behind the mythology references, which in a lot of cases seem to have been deliberately misspelled. He was a big believer in Jesus and also spoke of a man who would come from the 50th degree who may renew the weakened church.

Nostradamus' last name literally means "Our Lady,". His grandfather was from a long line of rabbinical scholars but converted from Judaism to Catholicism around 1455. He then changed the family name from Gassonet to Nostredame in obvious reference to Mary, mother of Jesus.

Nostradamus seems to have identified as a Messianic Jew—an ethnic Jew who accepts Jesus Christ as the Messiah. He describes his metaphysical experiences of entering a trance and being contacted by Michael the Archangel, which is where his knowledge of the future comes from. He also acknowledges that the information contained in his verses is dangerous and open to abuse by others. This explanation of his abilities mirrors my own in some ways and certainly expresses my sense of worry about how the information is used, especially when it is extracted by force. The biggest difference between our accounts is that I was lovingly and protectively embraced by a beautiful "goddess," who took a form of familiarity and comfort to me. She introduced me to Apollo, the culturally accepted personification of prophecy, human knowledge, and creativity. I know that my experience is unconventional and it cannot be easily linked to traditional ideas in the Abrahamic religions, but I am comforted by the fact that an incredibly famous, gifted, and widely accepted prophet professes a similar idea, most obviously in his name—Michael of the Holy Lady!

The Metatron

There were many virgin queens and goddesses in the ancient mythological worlds. I believe that the being who transported me to heaven to explain my ability and purpose through symbolism also correlates to some of these deities, especially the Jewish Metatron, the speaker for God, the lesser Yahweh, and the most powerful and pure of all the angels. I know that by most interpretations, the Metatron is a male or genderless spirit, but I believe—and most historians would agree—that women were removed from the Pantheon in almost every modern culture because of the pivot towards patriarchy with male-dominated clergy and priesthoods, demonstrated by the obvious preference for monarchs to be kings.

Although the Roman Church did retain the idea of the Holy Spirit, it did recognise many apparitions and supernatural visitations as the manifestations and communications of "Mary, Mother of God," "Holy Virgin," and "Blessed Mother." In my mind, it is far more believable that these phenomenal events were divine angelic encounters and attributed to Mary by church decree, who, in retrospect, assumed the likeness and identity of an ancient spiritual entity, inheriting the many titles formerly associated with the ancient goddesses of pre-history cultures. I am not a fan of the belief that human beings can be transformed into angels upon death, as in the cases of Enoch, Mary, or Jesus, or that angels can be transformed into humans to live a human life, but I am no authority on the matter—just an average human mind trying to logically analyse seemingly inhuman things and supernatural phenomena.

TRAUMA

The Delusion Begins

I have been through so much—mostly mentally, to be fair. I believe I saw almost thirty years of my life when I was just seven, and then again when I was ten, each time turning back into a seemingly normal and clueless child when being snapped back out from a trance and awoken in this narrow three-dimensional plane. But at 29, the information stuck, or at least elements of that experience could not be forgotten. I remembered so much that was hidden at the back of my brain; it was like a dream you can vaguely remember because you have forgotten the unrealistic and confusing details as it is not within the usual realm of normal life experience. It seemed as though my unawareness of my experiences being hypnotised is actually what was screaming at me all along. But when it all triggered at once, my adult mind was screaming as I watched it all play out like a movie in my mind. I was paralysed and powerless, unable to influence those events or stop those things from happening to me or the world.

Shock-induction hypnosis is incredibly dangerous, damaging, and must be especially detrimental to the development of a young mind. A true deep state of hypnosis is like only using the back of your brain, possibly where your emotions are processed, or your unconscious dreams come to life. The frontal lobe is where you process the world; it's where you interpret the pictures sent from your eyes, where you store and process language, how you navigate the three-dimensional spaces of physical reality, and how you interact with the material world. It's also where your physical memories begin before passing back to the middle of your brain, where longer-term memories are stored.

When this frontal cortex of your brain is switched off, essentially like it's asleep or unconscious, you bypass all the usual brain processes. You are blind and unaware of hot, cold, touch, facial expressions, light, movement, and even time. Memories are not stored and processed in the usual manner, and you are forced to rely on the senses that they say may become enhanced for a blind person. I felt more aware of some movements, other people's emotions or thoughts, their intentions, their tactics of manipulation, and I was especially conscious of their lies and the thinking behind them.

But this can be extremely damaging when you are being ambushed and coerced by people that you are uncomfortable around, when you do not know them, and you are being threatened with violence as they try to intimidate and control you. You are paralysed and blindfolded and they make it clear that they have all the power and expect you to beg for your life or pledge obedience. These people are purely trying to take from you and doing as much damage as they can in the process—psychological, emotional, and even intellectual damage—attempting to slow down your mind and make you believe lies and hear voices. They sneer at every true or factual statement while attempting to convince you that your truths are wrong. They want you to believe that their beliefs are more important and beneficial if you concur. They were trying to provoke me emotionally, make me psychologically aggressive, and afraid of physical violence, trying to force me into playing along with lies and deception or agreeing with their small-minded, self-interested, and false beliefs. They would offer friendship if you supported them, or conspiracy if you refused, wealth and power if you satisfied them, or poverty and outcast if you declined.

I stood my ground and stuck to my convictions, but every single time, they just wanted me to suffer for it. But I also understood that playing along or accepting falsities and mistruths was going to cause something much worse and for many more people.

Mental Suffering and A Fragmented Mind

Becoming conscious and not remembering these intense moments of fight or flight (hyperarousal or acute stress response) is unbelievably confusing. The basic human instinct in social settings is to play along and try to fit in with the group, pretending that you are not weak or bewildered, especially in an unfamiliar location or when surrounded by newly acquainted persons. Often, we just ignore the suspicious and try to break the ice for the sake of ourselves and our company, attempting to avoid a confrontation that might negatively impact the group psyche.

But as these memories came flooding back in the months that followed, I began to realise that my mind had been split for so very long. Hypnotising someone and putting them under intense strain develops their mind through short-term memory—we learn constantly, noting dangers and people or situations that are toxic to our development. But to be awakened and not recall, and being placed back at that moment when you thought you were safe, is massively damaging and leaves you liable to be coaxed back into a danger that your mind and memories should be warning you to avoid.

This essentially gives you two personalities that are in direct conflict: one who knows that you are in danger and is trying to warn you, and your primary personality who doesn't quite notice the gaps in his memory or the lost time. He is unaware, oblivious, and just trying to get along in life as if everything is normal—but it's not!

This theory also applies in another way. If you are hypnotised and learn some new information about your past, your enemies, your friends, your family, or the world, and then reawakened, that part of you that became slightly more knowledgeable, or aware and wiser, was suddenly lost or reset once more. When awakened and returned to "normality," you will continue on as normal attempting to be socially compatible with those around you but eventually finding that your mind can no longer adjust.

This was done to me numerous times at various stages of my development, multiple times in a row. Every time I caught them out on a lie or a mistruth, they would try to jumble my mind, as if trying to turn me into a zombie or a vegetative state of mind—making me receptive only to their commands. I never thought that I could witness or experience such extreme abuses of another person's mind, with the controller wanting their own self-beliefs to become real and widely accepted by those around them. I was treated like a toy, a crystal ball, or a genie that would be imprisoned and mistreated until I granted the fantasies of some very unhinged and dangerous people some form of realism and mirrored belief.

As this scenario played out in my conscious mind in the following months, I began to feel like the back of my mind had been screaming so loud and for so long because it wanted the front of my brain to hear it and understand what it had been missing. I had been hypnotised and awoken so many times, and at so many different stages in my early development, that I seemed to have multiple versions of my own mind and personality in a constant screaming match. It seems they were trying to share their individual memories with my confused and frustrated frontal-lobe conscious mind. It was difficult to accept, and even then, there was no way to deal with it or confront it—that time had long passed. Now it was a highly unusual, long-hidden, series of abnormal events far back in my past, but it was still deciding my future. I needed to challenge people to admit to, or be aware of, something that had never been acknowledged or widely recognised before.

I do not know a whole lot about the academic or scientific study of hypnosis. And my only experiences of it were taken away and hidden from me. I had done some reading, and there is some evidence that has linked it to potential triggers for auditory hallucinations—and that is when it is used professionally and responsibly. They say that anybody prone to or affected by schizophrenia should never go under. But given the way it was used on me, I think anybody would end up hearing independent voices they could not control. I think those people knew what they were doing. I believe they deliberately set out to make people, including myself, hear voices. I believe that they heard voices themselves, but worst of all, they were trying to convince their targets that it was a psychic ability, like hearing God. They claimed to be making people gifted.

It is another strategy of abusers and manipulators trying to evade detection and avoid being confronted—a way of making your victims depend on you, convincing them that no one else would ever understand, or that if you tried to report your experiences, the government health services would lock you away instead and dose you with medications for the rest of your life, labelling your memories as inaccurate false beliefs. "You'd be better off with us" was a common phrase of theirs. So now, I felt like I had to challenge the whole system. I had dealt with my experiences all alone for a very long time, so I was confident that I could articulate my ideas about the causes relatively well.

I did seek out talking therapy with government psychologists. And I spoke about many of my broken and jumbled experiences. I did not say that I thought I might be Jesus Christ, but I did say that the people hypnotising me seemed to believe that I could tell the future and were asking me very specific questions. I used Nostradamus and Edgar Cayce as a kind of case study—examples of men who were said to enter a trance voluntarily and without any exterior triggers, who then received and communicated knowledge of the future. They were far more receptive than I had expected.

I also paid for private hypnotherapy, mostly to discuss my experiences of hypnosis and request some professional industry opinion on its weaponisation. He did give me some therapy, but it was mostly ambient vocal guidance to relax my body and mind—not the same type of deep-state hypnosis that I had experienced so many times before. I did find that the hypnotherapy session helped me to feel more relaxed than I had felt in years. I also discussed the "anti-therapy" that was used on me—I was brainwashed into overeating and smoking more, made restless and hyperactive, sleepless and manic, less confident and anxious—everything you might go to a therapist to cure. They were using every method available to try to make me sick, unhealthy, mentally and emotionally beset, and they wanted me to hate myself. Every single thing that they ever did to me was maliciously fixated on causing maximum damage, every single word or action was intended to shorten my life and vandalise my mind, body, and spirit. It was the most selfishly egotistical escapade that I have ever heard of. They have truly tried anything and everything that they could possibly think of and would have done much worse if they were sure they could escape retribution. I was honestly treated like something they were trying to demolish—not a person, not a human, but simply an object that was blocking their preferred and intended path.

Not quite all of the answers that I needed or wanted, but at least there were some. No-one in my actual social circle acknowledged my experiences at all. But it was surely known all along, long before I became aware of it. I mean, the longer you lie to someone, the more likely it is that you will never tell them the truth and you will become even more aggressive and outrageous to avoid or deny that fact. I'm not the type to try and force my will on anyone. If they want to lie or pretend, so be it!

Enoch And Samyaza

I began to feel like I had triggered the events that would slowly destroy the world. My gift had been misused; the world was in chaos, conflicts spilling across borders. The world had been in perpetual crisis since I turned 19, and with the events currently unfolding in Palestine, I was now watching the apocalypse on live stream.

I was feeling very much like the real-life version of The Book of Enoch. The story of Enoch and Samyaza is said to have been recorded in Jerusalem and Ethiopia between 400 B.C. and 100 A.D. Samyaza was a Watcher angel who was sent down to earth to share God's knowledge with mankind. He then abused his status to start wars and sow chaos. He taught man psychological warfare, science, and how to manufacture weapons and armour. He gave the daughters of men half-angel offspring and unfurled the tentacles of corruption across the world.

Enoch was a prophet and a saint, Noah's grandfather, who was said to have been taken to Heaven without dying, to save him from the coming apocalypse. These chaotic and ruinous events are suggested to be the main catalyst for God's wrath during the time of Noah, when he sent the flood to cleanse the world of the corruption and destruction that had spread like wild hellfire.

I felt like both of these characters. My gift was the conduit for the "knowledge of the Angels," which had been ambushed by men who abused it because they wanted to be gods on Earth. But I am supposed to be more like Enoch—pure and selfless, honest and true. I had become the plot device of a movie about mental illness, with intensely attentive followers who only obey when you tell them to do the wrong thing, and who strive to interrupt or sabotage everything that you might do for yourself or for others who are not them.

These "followers" made a point of going against everything I wanted for myself and only seemed to want me to be what I am when I am "asleep," They never cared at all for who I am or what I wanted out of life. They swore that they would "kill everything I love."

In so many ways, they had tried to brainwash me and make me like them, wanting me to do the thinking for them. But I wasn't like them. This ability saved me every bit as much as it had made me the target

for some of the worst elements in this world, and I was determined
to hold true.

ACCEPTANCE

The Invisible Prison

Most of my life, I have been extremely passive. I would have considered myself to be casual and easy-going, priding myself on being nonconfrontational, nonviolent, and receptive to other people's freedom and individuality. This also means that at times, I have allowed myself to be taken advantage of, bullied into silence, or have gone along with the crowd in situations I was unsure of. It can be difficult to know yourself growing up when you are surrounded by so many distractions and variety in a world that is swarming with uniqueness and many separate individuals pulling you in numerous different directions.

At certain times throughout my life, there were always people around me deliberately trying to upset my inner peace and self-belief. There were plenty of times when I felt that the bully tactics were specifically tuned to target my own personal well-being and sense of individual freedom of choice and self-determination. However, I refused to spend too much time overthinking it or allowing others to upset my sense of inner strength or quiet confidence. Still, I was under the impression that we would all eventually move on or grow together. I was unaware of the depth of some people's commitment to holding me in place and using every piece of my mind and my life to enhance their own.

I never truly understood how those around me acted so strangely and, at times, were so focused on personal attacks and overstepping intimate boundaries. They could be nice and friendly to coax me out but would then turn into tormentors and oppressors when there were more people around to witness it. At first, I thought this was just immaturity, but the older we got, the worse it became, and the more I felt like my life was a theatre or stage play that was under someone else's direction.

By the time I was sixteen and nineteen, I was invited to hang out with my local friends, and as soon as the greetings and niceties were out of the way, they would shout obscenities or make derogatory comments but then behave as if nothing happened. If I tried to confront them, either in front of the group or on a more personal basis, they would deny what had taken place and then carry on as normal, but just a few minutes later, they would repeat their strange outbursts and comments. Eventually, I would fall into permanent silence and ignore their unnatural behaviour. Unfortunately for me, there was no way to force a truthful discussion.

It would be years until I understood what this "insane" and socially challenging psychological warfare tactic actually is: gas lighting. Denial of truth, twisting reality, and pretending that you are confused or "paranoid" are all tricks employed by manipulators and con artists. I never realised that it was ever practiced on a scale like this or initiated as a mode of control over someone who was completely unaware of their own value. I was the subject of a very obvious conspiracy, but I truly had no idea why. I never would have guessed the true nature of its source or purpose.

The Blood Moon

I was led into a trap. In fact, many traps, many times, but I did not recall or understand until my brain matured, and I fell victim to the same trap once more. This was such a strange experience, and the realisation at first was ridiculous and absurd, but as I searched for more answers both deep inside and far outside of myself, I began to absorb the fundamentals, and the idea became unbearable, tragic, terrorising, and extraordinarily traumatising, because it started to seem logical. In reality, it was the only thorough explanation for all the questions that I so desperately needed an answer to.

I almost completely broke down. I had believed that I was him for around three years. I felt hated and isolated, scammed and conned. I was an easy target, betrayed and spied on, manipulated and abused in so many different ways. I was helpless and without any power or independence, with no platform or arena to discuss the chasmic and enigmatic meanings behind this comforting, yet strangely unsettling and unnerving presence. I felt so truly alone. Almost. I still had God, but I also had the books and his words, his prophecies, his direction, and his truth. But I wasn't sure that I could even understand it or trust it, especially if those words have been rewritten or corrupted, misused by the many emperors and kings, or the clergymen, generals, and upper classes that have taken precedence over all others throughout the ages.

I knew I was him, but I could never be sure that I was the "one" from prophecy, and even if I was, it could still be a very regrettable outcome. And besides, how could there be one when he is many? Then came the tetrad, four blood moons in around eighteen months. I was stressed and conflicted, unsure of my place in the world or if my fate was always to be the victim of violence and false belief. I saw all four of those full blood moons. I watched them all from home, saw them across the hills behind my house, but the final one was special somehow. I felt so calm and at peace, for what seemed like the first time ever. The moon was completely dark and had a true "blood" red colour. I was thirty-three and finally accepted what I/he/we am, are, was, and is. I am not sure what we or I can or will be, but I do not seek to control or decide all that will come to pass. I am him. I accepted that, at long last.

But something else truly blew my mind, something that came after for me but was written so very long before. It was probably almost ten years later when I reread the original prophecies of Nostradamus—"The new sage with the lone brain, sees the moon above the high mountain." It was so surreal, a private moment that was so solitary and which I had never mentioned to anyone, described so poignantly in a five-hundred-year-old book, written by a man that I already knew was one of him. I was elated and felt elevated for the first time. My first experience of someone telling the truth about him and me.

The Ram's Head

I am an Aries, and although I do not give too much significance to modern astrology, I do believe that there were significantly noteworthy celestial alignments approximately a couple of months either side of my birth date. I was born between the entire solar planetary "Grand Alignment" of March 1982 and a total lunar eclipse which was also classed as a super blue blood moon.

I do understand now that there are actually many prophetic references to me—almost too many to recall. Many may have not yet been fulfilled but most seem to be associated with marks of identity. He has been missing for such a long time so it may be more about knowledge and awareness or a return to recognition and understanding rather than miracles or thrones and crowns or empire. But I do also think it is more about the times that I live in than the person that I am: trials and tribulations, trumpets, dragons casting falling stars from the skies, broken seals on age-old prophecy, biblical numbers and signs, and omens for all mankind.

I do believe that we are entering a dangerous era for man. We have the power to destroy ourselves, and even to sterilise the Earth forever, creating an environment that no advanced lifeform could survive or evolve in. Technology is becoming stale for ordinary people and their way of life, but not for military spyware and weapons, giving fewer and fewer people more and more power. If we can survive the next two hundred years without trying to destroy each other or the world in the process, or become victims of our own madness and greed, or using a great power that no man should have, I am confident that we can live for as long as the Earth can support us.

I do so hope that we have the courage and conviction to ensure that the earth can live much longer than we will, as this may be our true test and our most likely failing. We must do our best to guarantee that the world can support all forms of life for many generations after our own lifetimes. This should be our priority as a society. The economy is not real; money has no value (outside of our economic system); war can only destroy, and peace can only come with maturity. Food, water, shelter, and peace is all that we really need to survive. Everything else is just cosmetic! Please keep this in mind when we threaten war and destruction on our neighbours and brothers, and by extension, ourselves.

SPOOKY ACTION AT GREAT DISTANCE

The Messianic Anomaly

There are some incredibly outlandish and inexplicable ideas in physics: black holes, wormholes, white holes, quantum entanglement, the overlapping dimensions of a multiverse, and even an "anti-universe," parallel and identical to our own but where time and its lifecycle run backward. I think all of those theoretical, unproven and unfathomable ideas can actually help describe and explain the messianic gift.

Black holes disrupt the flow of time. They absorb matter and potentially spew out condensed information through a wormhole or white hole which resides at a different location in space-time. The messianic gift could be vaguely discussed as a wormhole or white hole because he sees the future as something that could be described as interactive holograms and can communicate some of that newly acquired information that comes from a different location in space time, with his audience in the present. He may also be unintentionally sending some of that information back into the past where our ancestors have proven their knowledge of us.

He might also be described as being quantum entangled with the Creator and original singularity giving him awareness of the parallel dimensions of time which he can remote-view using his mind or spirit. He may also be entangled on a quantum level with his genetic line of avatars which might help to explain their spiritual connection and ability to share information or siphon it into the past or present from their future selves. It is an incredibly difficult and multifaceted situation that may never have a complete scientific explanation—such as being in two places at once through incorporeal time travel, or being used as a spyglass for men that reside in another dimension of time, far, far back in the past.

I feel as though it carries me forward, far out into the deepest hidden dimensions of existence. I am merely a passenger, documenting as much important and useful information as humanly possible. There were times when I used his gift and felt like I was falling into a black hole, and time had stopped. At the same time, I felt like time was moving so fast that I could not hold onto the information I was being exposed to and could only describe each event once before that moment had passed me by, and I was suddenly somewhere else further along on my path through the timeline.

We are a very young civilisation and society, on the cusp of understanding a much larger and interconnected reality than we ever thought possible. The rarest and most supernatural of human occurrences is actually an ever-present and endlessly looping one, and his mind is an important receiver and transmitter that connects us all, throughout this multiverse of simultaneous realities which exist in separate dimensions of time.

The Black Star

At the beginning of time, a black or inverted star-like object suddenly expanded, shredding itself down to its most basic constituent components. It was a singular mass which was virtually infinitely divisible, giving it the ability to split itself into many pieces that were in many ways identical to their parent, except they were faster, lighter, and more energised.

This is how our universe was born. Technically, we are still inside that object; its borders just expanded to allow space to exist between many of its basic elements. Many of these minuscule parts slowly recombined to form supermassive stars that quickly collapsed into black holes, and their cores became the gravity-well galactic centres that holds galactic material together. These supernovae implosions caused these first transient stars to eject their outer layers and seed the new world of worlds with both heavy and light elements, paving the way for medium-sequence, long-life, stable stars to form, along with their satellite planetary systems.

The original singularity became everything in the new world, including its very fabric, space-time. Everything in the universe seems to follow exactly the same patterns because the same inexplicable force governs them. The universe behaves as though it was designed around a single prototype and then replicated that behaviour on both macro and micro scales. Similar to a theoretical self-programmed machine repeating its behavioural code because it has been optimised and refined to perfection, as it strives toward equilibrium—the perfect balance of all its competing dominant forces.

The Eye of Providence

I feel that this original singular object still exists out there somewhere, far back in the timeline (and maybe forward), still in its true form. It had the ability to transform itself into space and time, every known and unknown element, light, and a type of immensely gravitational material from which nothing can escape, except maybe radiation. This original form is the basis for everything, and in a way, everything in the universe is still orbiting that object as it gradually reconstitutes itself over trillions of years.

The behaviour of everything in the universe is based on the interaction of many smaller replicas of this original form. They are all following along on a predetermined path that can ultimately have only one outcome—collision. This pattern will repeat over and over until the end of time and will finish with the eventual collapse of everything in existence.

Pieces of this original object is what we are all made from. We can only move in certain directions on this earthly plane, just as organisms follow waves of energy and patterns of invisible frequency as a scaffold to construct cells, limbs, trees, and everything organic in nature. We call these organic proportions the golden ratio or the Fibonacci sequence, but we are still not sure exactly why it is the precise ratio that it seems to be. I would interpret this as a cosmic law or blueprint, a pattern that everything naturally obeys. But where these basic forms of life get the information from to evolve and arrange themselves into such complex mosaics is another great mystery that we will never fully understand.

The original object is what every atom was once an inseparable part of. Hence, we are all still connected to it because we are made from the pieces of it. In my mind, that means the reason this object might know all or see all is because it is all. Sometimes it feels like an infinitely black eye is watching over us. And we are merely just an extension or an expression of it—as if we are all still within its borders and can never escape it's line of sight. We are merely miniscule and seemingly independent parts of its reality and existence. To me, that suggests that it wants us to know it, just as much as it knows us. And I do think that interpretation translates very well to the behaviour of an immortal information-based mechanical lifeform, endlessly replicating and reproducing, and is without time, or death or desire, but is threaded with logic, balance, truth, and conscious omnipresence.

In a great many ways it seems as though we were all ejected from that 4- or 5-dimensional black hole, but we are being pushed or falling toward another one. One exists at the beginning of time, while the other will form at the end, when the cycle begins anew.

Is it possible that these black stars are somehow moving backwards through time? And at some distant point in the universe's lifecycle, they will all begin to coalesce, overpowering the expansion of space and the speed of light as they gather pace and mass, and when there are no opposing forces or similar objects left to counter its dominance, even space-time itself will begin to fall backwards into complete collapse.

Is Time Moving Backwards, Or Is My Mind Falling Forward?

It is difficult to understand how any human mind could see forward through time. Is time moving backwards, or is he part of an information superhighway that is propelled forward through ethereal dimensions of physical time that we have not experienced yet? This situation with him (me and the other versions of him) proves that the future does, in fact, affect the past, and the past has the ability to affect the present in real time, but only under certain conditions, such as recording and sharing information that acts as a time capsule. Reading a book by Nostradamus or exploring Muhammad's hadith has certainly affected my frame of mind and my plan of action. I know that these people have changed most and possibly all of us, but I believe that he may be calling me to respond and trigger some part of our collective destiny.

I think I understand some of what needs to be done, but I am still trying to figure out how to make that happen. I feel like there are many who are trying to stop me, and even more who are trying to use me to collect his and our "inheritance" for themselves. Life has been so difficult trying to figure out what I am supposed to do, or if anyone would ever accept whatever that is meant to be. I spent the last number of years feeling trashed and stomped on, as if Palestine were the only ones who wanted or needed him, while everyone else just took what they could and then pretended he did not exist.

An Overpowered Monster in A Weak Human Mind

I am very much at odds with the ways of the world and the ability that I have come to know so well. How has this overpowered monster possessed my life? History made him into the centre of a world that I have been made to feel I don't belong in. I do believe in the purpose of this gift and its potential to transform society and the world. But at the same time, it is a lot of pressure to fall onto one tiny human, and it seems like a terrible idea to depend solely on one person to do so much or be expected to overpower so many.

I would not want to enforce compliance concerning any of my ideals. If the planet is in danger because of us, then maybe that is just the nature of life and its narrow window for advanced progress. Realistically, we really should try harder to pay it forward and save ourselves, each other, and our descendants. There will be an end someday, and it is inevitable, unless we can travel throughout the galaxy or move the Earth to a cooler location when the sun becomes smaller, hotter, and more unstable but even that is just buying time. I expect that eventually we will have to learn to accept the cosmic fate of our place in the world. We can find peace and comfort in the knowledge of God and the belief in our inevitable return to life on another world or in a different version of this universe. And I hope that we can depend on each other, no matter what the future holds. We are all in this together until we learn how to become as one.

The Genetic Line of Prophethood

There is a popular video game franchise that simulates the idea of genetic memory. The plot centres around a futuristic machine that aids the user in exploring the memories and life experiences of our ancestors which are somehow stored in our DNA. I found this concept incredibly fascinating and have given it much thought over the years. I do not think that I can experience the challenges of Muhammad (PBUH), or the travels of Nostradamus, but it is a strange sentiment to feel that they might have had the ability to explore my mind or existence, study the world that I live in, or analyse my life and trials. They have even influenced my journey into possibly becoming something more and encouraging my commitment to an action of conceivably great significance.

They have spoken about me like they knew me. Nostradamus also wrote things like "his disciples invite him to be immortal." I have collapsed under the weight of it all. Because of my own experiences, I have doubted their suggestions of followers and loyalty, but I have slowly begun to realise something. In a funny sort of way, I am his disciple, so maybe, somehow, he is also mine. It is he who spoke to me from throughout the ages and described parts of my life, or some of the things on my mind. And in many ways, they really did save me from madness and despair. But they also need me—to make good on their promise, to fulfil their collective destiny and immortal promise, to express a complex understanding of our combined purpose, and hopefully, to change the world for the better.

There does seem to be a kind of telepathic link between us. I know that their words are open to interpretation, and even most of Nostradamus' quatrains could be easily taken as schizophrenic nonsense and deluded ramblings. Or so heavily encrypted with ambiguous references that they are meant to be vague with application to almost any event. But there is something powerful and wise in what he wrote. There is logic, purpose, and pattern. Genetically, I am part Jew but I am also part French and since I have this ability, and it has been described as a line that passes along males from the House of David, the pattern becomes very suggestive of the possibility that I may just be his direct descendant. That could explain our seemingly strong connection and his multiple quatrains that place a lot of emphasis on the same person and events. And I believe we all want and need his story to be told, and to free our minds from idolatry and false belief or from the wolves who dress as sheep.

Behavioural Patterns

I think that in a lot of ways the universe is like an independent, self-written computer program, and we are all individual programs trying to understand our creator, fulfilling an important part of God's nature and purpose.

I would imagine that this essence, this spiritual ability and prophetic gift, might also function rather like a semi-conscious and sometimes automatic computer program. It is capable of collecting, processing, and expressing complex information, which is then copied or replicated by his copies (us). Then in one of his next incarnations, he returns to his descendants who would then act as a source of recorded information or a knowledge bank, reabsorbing the stored data, checking the knowledge for errors, truths, or corruption, then restating those facts and instructions in shorter, truer statements. This repeated behaviour would have an important function in streamlining valuable data, making it more efficient and easier to share, store, or process. The ultimate goal being adding more knowledge and universal truths while improving the language of instruction and people's understanding of its source, along with its system of reasoning.

Genetics behaves in this manner too, consistently trying to shed old information and code or allowing it to become inactive, enhancing stronger, more advantageous traits and attributes, ensuring survival and efficiency, and benefiting the entire colony.

A Monkey on a Floating Rock

I get the sense sometimes that this journey we share, this path that we all walk together, is the greatest story never told, given how we are taught and conditioned to see the world as though we are surrounded by enemies or at risk of faltering if we let our guard down. I feel like that is such a pointless and defeatist exercise and truly only benefits those who already hold power and wealth.

I do get some silly images in my mind, but strangely still, it usually is an odd expression of a contradictory truth. I imagine that man awoke some five or ten million years ago, becoming aware of himself and his environment.

Not nearly a human but not quite an animal either. Realising he was different and was growing the capacity to understand why or how, he did choose to be different, every bit as much as it happened all by itself. It has taken us an eternity to wander the earth, observe and measure its clockwork mechanics, and communicate in ways we never thought possible.

And just when we thought we knew it all, the time has come for another awakening. I truly hope that we can discover true peace along this journey with him. I know that it is work, and I understand that we are afraid, but we must accept our awareness and feel closer to God. I would say that this is the most frightening and terrifying thing that has ever existed. It is an understanding that you are insignificant, and the universe will eventually consume and recycle you in the most overpowered way imaginable. But the universe does not forget; it stores everything, and no information can ever truly be destroyed. Everything we do matters. It is recorded by the light we emit as it fills the universe. There is much more to life, existence, and consciousness than what we see with our eyes, and beyond anything we could ever hope to know with our minds.

And that could only mean that awareness of God is about finding peace, gaining a deeper understanding of the world, and sensing our transformed and evolved purpose. It is about building a better world—not just for ourselves but for our descendants—so that we can return to this world as someone brand new, someone who never existed before, and maybe even on the opposite side of the world, among the very people that we once believed could only be our enemies.

The Holistic System

A holistic system occurs when a number of individual parts or specifically engineered devices are interconnected or assembled bringing about the emergence of a brand-new system with distinct ability. This new capability is one which is not inherent to any of the particular elements but arises when the components synchronise and begin to function as one. Whether that's an engine or a computer or a network of computers, the sum of all the parts, when assembled in a compatible configuration, becomes greater than its individual components.

Technically humans have a similar function. One man may be weak, but many are powerful. And a sea of people could move mountains if we so willed it.

We are consistently extending our abilities through intellect, machinery, supercomputers, interconnectedness, and synchronicity. When we work together, we are incredibly beneficial to each other, and potentially even the Earth and its environment. But when we resist each other or clash, we are massively destructive, dangerous, and lethal.

The sum of us all is a godlike force and a borderless, undefined object, especially now that we are so many. And for so long we have been unaware that we have become this unbalanced force of nature that has no equal or opposite. We have changed the earth, redirected rivers, flattened forests, subjugated the world's fauna, and transformed our atmosphere to a potential crisis point.

If we are to defeat our own aggressive nature, we must all fit together for something else to emerge as part of a new system. So that we can conquer, not the natural world, nor the animal kingdom, but our own beastly nature. And awareness of ourselves, our environment, and our collective future has the potential to transform us into something brand new and unexpected.

The White Horseman

Some say that the horsemen represent the end, but I am not so sure. They could also represent our awareness of it, and our ability to destroy ourselves if we continue to behave recklessly and selfishly. The horseman of death is the most ambiguous of the story's powerful imagery. If death was also the white horseman, our supposed saviour and guide, he could only be Jesus, the reincarnated prophet, the man who somehow conquered death and is ritually returned to life. The man who may have already seen the end, right at the very beginning, and has been trying to comfort us—and himself— ever since. I would say that he has known true terror and dread and has had to keep reliving that, praying that he can change it. As we become aware of our own immortality, knowing when and where it all began, we will become more aware of our mortality, understanding how it all might end, or how often it may have happened before.

Revelations and The Global Empire

The first horseman was white and carried a bow and crown, conquering a quarter of the earth—an allegory that aligns with his modern origins in Sumer, Egypt, Jerusalem, and India. The bow may represent our hunter gatherer origins and the evolution from small nomadic groups to settlers and city dwellers.

The second is red, carrying a great sword, conquering another quarter of the world through war. This description fits the empires of Rome, Greece, and Mongolia, and even the modern nations of Britain and America, that marched across the map to extend their territories, amassing wealth and infamy.

The third was black and held a pair of scales, possibly representing trade and economy, conquering a further quart. The verse describes men who work all day just for the price of a meal. I think this is symbolic of the economic model that has come from medieval monarchy, colonisation, and capitalism. Ethiopia, Sudan, Palestine—so many have suffered from malnutrition and scarcity, not because there is not enough food in the world, but because the global economy is designed around enriching and empowering the corporations and capitalists, not providing for all the people of the world. We have plundered and pillaged Africa, the Americas, and Asia. We are all horsemen.

And then comes the pale, who, in some interpretations, raises the dead and is followed by Hades. This one is much more difficult to understand, but he is also described as being the first and the last—holding the keys to death and Hades. This could mean that he is the first king and prophet, returned and resurrected but on a quest to honour the victims of the cruel systems of power that we have spread across the Earth, one continent at a time.

Combined, we really are a mighty force—marching forward through time, back and forth across the earth for over five million years. We are all incredibly powerful. We have done great things, but it almost always has a hefty cost. I hope we can find ways to negate that in the future as we drift through time and hurtle through space, hopefully accepting that we cannot possess or control everything in the realm. We all deserve a fair share in this system of procurement, provision, and division.

The Empires of old began as independent city-states that rose and fell and occasionally collided, conquered, and collapsed before the cycle began again. Nowadays, empires don't so much collapse as pulsate, growing in political or economic might before their waning when the same type of influence would again begin to grow outward as it emanates from within another territory.

Gog and Magog (Yajuj and Majuj)

These stories appear in many cultures and have had many interpretations and associations throughout the millennia. They were spoken about by Ezekiel, Daniel, Muhammad (PBUH), and also in the Book of Revelations (written by "John" but probably inspired by Jesus). There must be numerous different meanings involved with these stories as they were told by so many independent prophets at various times since at least 500 BCE. Some believe that these prophecies have been fulfilled while others think that they are more closely related to the ideas surrounding a great Satan that is periodically captured and bound in the abyss only to be released at certain times and aligning with various events in human history. They could also be interpreted as the twin beasts in Revelations, when one is defeated, another identical form rises to snatch power once more.

I have given these stories much thought, and although I am not a scholar or educated to a significant degree, I do sense that if I am what I "know" myself to be I should be capable of valued insight into these suspected repeating events. Historically, the world has had many empires with violent and ruthless clashes that have had destructive and poisonous results. Some of the worst events have involved mighty, heavily armed and organised armies targeting unarmed civilians and stealing from working-class people. This is a serious abuse of power and is more like organised crime than civilised empire.

I would also think that parts of these stories could represent the modern borders where West meets East and North meets South. Global society has begun to fracture over the last number of years after much progress and integration. The same nations have had almost all of the power for many centuries. With the rise of America and two world wars the globe has underwent fundamental change. European powers drew the borders in the Middle East and Africa with the intent of keeping people divided and countries weak. With the end of British colonisation, many are still adjusting while trying to develop and stabilise. Now with the rise of China and a potential economic alliance across the global south, the world will change again.

Every nation around Israel is in complete chaos and it's all because of their decade's long actions in Palestine. The recent events have further divided global politics and even civil societies, but it has become clear that America has too much power on the world stage, and Israel will never negotiate with anybody. People want an honest and true resolution, but there appears to be zero appetite for peace and prosperity with the current balance of power.

The world is now one place, and any event that occurs in one territory will immediately affect every other region. Most powerful states have coalesced with many others and this has resulted in major military and economic powerhouses encroaching, overlapping, and triggering proxy warfare rather than direct confrontation. The older economic model destroyed, fragmented, and impoverished half the world and most are only now becoming seemingly independent with many still suffering and underdeveloped.

These forms of indirect warfare are most evident in parts of Africa, Palestine, Syria, Afghanistan, Iran, Taiwan, and Ukraine. The peoples of these territories tend to be mixed culturally and sometimes genetically. This can have the effect of nations being divided between competing or aligning empires who employ underhanded tactics to spark chaos, collapse, civil unrest, right-wing violence, or coups. Sometimes civil conflicts are based more on majority culture attempting to remove outliers or "foreign" traditions and heritage. This usually arises through politics that no longer tolerates difference and seeks to empower itself through aggression. All peoples should be accepted, especially those of mixed heritage and values. We can no longer afford to spread chaos and divide nations as we compete to trounce our neighbours in the hope of empowering our leaders and enriching our economies while many more are impoverished and disenfranchised.

The Numbered Beast

When I realised that I could tell the future, and had been ambushed by criminals who acted like agents of the empire's hidden underbelly, it made me think a lot about the empire of the beast and what that means for me/him. These days we are all born with birth certificates, family names, addresses, phone numbers, and many other forms of unique identification.

This brought me to the conclusion that this spirit and gift no longer has anywhere left to hide. But that also means in this age of information and interconnection the empire can no longer hide either. No matter who he is or where he comes from, he will no longer be helping to build brand-new empires or inspire unique religions. Instead he will have to try to improve on what we already have and amalgamate the best parts from each of our cultures, if that really is our collective destiny and acceptable to global society.

We are all better informed and educated in these times. The ruling classes no longer have the same level of intellectual advantage that they had once upon a time. We all have a realistic grasp on history, psychology, and the methods of wealth accumulation and power preservation. We all have equal shares in this world and it is up to each and every one of us to ensure that this earth is somewhere we want to return to—as any random member of global society. That is what I am aiming for and I know that is what he would want too. Society will never be fully equal or completely fair. We all have different talents and unequal value in the economy. But a corrupt system that rewards advantage to the wrong people ultimately hurts us all and erodes everyone's faith in the system itself. We should all have a chance to change the world for the better and I pray we can work together to make every society something that we all want to play a part in.

MANY GODS FROM ONE TRUE FORM

I feel sometimes that there exist many gods as aspects of the one true God and the many realities it creates. I think so much about all the books of knowledge and the laws that they express, our nature and its purpose, our spirits and our consciousness. I know the fear we feel when we become more aware of our limitations and expiry. We are all part of an immortal organism that never really dies and could be over three billion years old. There may be a god-like collective consciousness and shared spirit, and we are the many lifeforms it possesses, with eight billion unique beings marching forward through time and colonising the planet as it becomes more consciously aware of itself.

The universe is launching us forward and slowly revealing its secrets, becoming so advanced and eternal that it is both observing itself and being observed. We are aware that we are being watched and guided by our ancestors, and they are aware of us. But we can become so afraid, anxious about the end, conscious of our limited window for existence, and apprehensive knowing that someday even the universe itself will collapse into a singularity and time itself will definitively cease to exist.

There is so much symbolism in his story, and in a way, he represents both life and death—we are the sons of the primordial or darkness and death itself, still somehow carrying a piece of the original and directly connected to the eternal object that exists beyond time and space, and in at least one dimension it never was destroyed and still has dominion and authority over time and all that exists within. It has imparted that gift of complex knowledge and awareness of its mysterious source unto us. And the daughter of life and light, navigating this three-dimensional plane of existence, multiplying exponentially, gathering knowledge and wisdom, and passing it on to the next generation.

We Are More Than 3D

We are all different parts of many great and wondrous, vastly encompassing, ghostly and material objects that defy true explanation or definite boundaries. This consciousness we all carry is a great unbroken and ever-changing knowledge bank that is hundreds of thousands of years old (at least). A genetic code that began between two and four billion years ago (LUCA). And a great spiritual presence that imparts us with wisdom and expresses heavenly compassion and altruistic intent, and is at least as old as the visible universe. And something else that is even older, predating time and existence, a seemingly self-aware mechanical organism and energy-based lifeform, which is in perpetual motion and cannot ever be lost or destroyed, or ever come to a stop.

I feel so connected to that primordial presence that, at times, I felt like I could see existence from an aerial view or through a panoramic lens. In many ways, it appears that the universe is just an uneven number that will always continue to throw itself out of balance, like a great and ample force that can never rest. Expressed through an unending matrix of choices, which, once made, will always lead to multiple more options—or a definitive answer that will ultimately pose many more questions.

His Story

Altogether, there are patterns in his story that seem to repeat: a "priesthood" that becomes too powerful, independent, and compartmentalised from broader society, or his bloodlines becoming corrupt or imprisoned and enslaved. A group of men who lust after him because they want to be him, they want to possess him and hold onto him, and they want him to come from them. It is a strange and powerful story—they have chased him across time, imprisoned him, killed him, and turned him into their throne and their symbol of ultimate power.

There are so many oddities at play around him. He is of a mixed race who, in some respects, appear to have become racist or classist. Some may even try to force him to share his blood with them. He wants us all to become something different, while they might use the blood of his newest avatars to turn themselves into something "new." It has become akin to a cat-and mouse game—he tries to escape, but they continue to follow him. He wants to change, but they want to remain the same.

In so many ways, that's not the whole story, but there certainly are, and always were, elements of those patterns amongst his oldest and closest "followers." His spirit seems to wander from tribe to tribe. It is a captivating and enchanting tale of a reincarnated man who manages to return in a different race or tribe but is still of the same original line. I think that says so much about genetic assimilation and interaction, and even the spiritual preference for genetic diversity. We will always seek to restore lost knowledge while exploring and expressing the new. He will always be a mix of many parts that have come from the same original but have gathered something extra along their journey through time and space.

The beginning of our early human hybrid and hominid story is also about mixing and interbreeding. In prehistory, progenitor primates became separated, branching into related species. But somehow they were forced back together to amalgamate upon another land assimilating into a brand new species before branching off again in multiple directions. This has happened over and over for millions of years, and considering his modern origins and the story of his mixed blood, I do believe that racism is a nonsense concept and true evolution is about us continually becoming one race, unafraid to mix and become something new and different—

something that may carry the best traits from all of our sister tribes. And if genetic memory is as plausible as spiritual time travel, who knows what we might discover if he wandered the earth once more, collecting and assimilating the genetic material he has long been separated from.

The Man Who Rose From a Sea Of People

Sometimes I wonder if all of the historical man-made tragedies were actually set in motion by our ancestors, who lacked a true understanding of humanity, the natural world, and the behaviour of the universe. Who then made the choices along the way? Were we simply following along the path of least resistance, as if everything was already laid out for them, and they merely stayed on the straight and narrow, the easiest track with the most obvious outcome and most self-serving result? Have we all been manipulated and corralled into a predetermined outcome? What is the beast? Is it a system of rules that we all obey? Are some allowed to use that system to cheat the many and benefit the few? Is any human actually in control, or are we all just going along with the crowd, or doing everything that we can get away with? If true, that truly is a mindless beast, with no morals, or conscience, and no way to be tamed.

I often wonder how my gift might have manifested had I not been hypnotised and lied to from such a young age. I feel so incredibly misled and have been conditioned to live in a false reality that was created by modern spies with a Dark Age mentality. This modern world was built on the foundations of a Stone Age civilisation, ruled by dishonest "priests" and "divine" kings with designs on ruling the world through the most brutal methods possible. Even the financial system was designed in the Middle Ages, and we are still manipulated into never questioning it's authority or doubting its legitimacy.

This thing I carry, which seems almost like a piece of God—an ability that only He should possess—has become such a large part of what I am that it has completely overtaken and transcended who I thought I was or could have been. I feel that I have been overwritten or deleted, and now I can only be some version of him, trying to fulfil his duties, make good on his word, while still on a quest to discover and reveal the many hidden truths of our collective coexistence.

This ability is peculiar, bizarre, frightening, and independently automatic, yet overwhelmingly profound and deeply fascinating. I do not want to be locked into an endless argument or power struggle with governments, royal clans, classists, racists, mafia, or clergymen. This overpowered ability seems to be so far outside of what any human could or should be, it is reaching forward all the time and yearns to connect with every living thing. There were times when it felt a little like a hive mind or some sort of interdimensional nexus point, and in a lot of ways it is. But I am merely one tiny human and this super-powered monster I have inside appears to be a far greater spiritual force than all of us combined. It is an almighty beast but it only want true peace and harmony, progress and unity, knowledge and wisdom, truth and justice, love and respect, order and balance, and glory for all.

We were not meant to be gods, or superior to each other. We are meant to work together, in synchronicity, aiding each other in becoming a natural and organic expression of our environment, complementing it in every way that we can—mimicking even the most basic organisms. That is the meaning of life, and the more misled and separated we become from our most basic function, the more we will disrupt the harmonious equilibrium of life's true nature, shorten the lifespan of our species, and even of the earth itself. We have to think as though we are holistic parts of this Earth's raw nature, as if we are still forming and growing in its fruitful womb, extending our abilities through science, knowledge, collaboration, and cooperation.

I would hope that our modern world can fit perfectly into the ecosystem with some very long-sighted adjustments. Knowledge, empire, and technology all come from God. It is our connection to His wisdom that gives us these virtually limitless abilities. It is part of who we are and what made us, and is the most basic interpretation of what the Messiah actually is and what he can help us to achieve. But we must heed the warnings and care for the world as if she were our own delicate offspring—as much as we are hers.

THE CHIRON

The Chiron is an unusual and unique character in the Greek mythological pantheon. His father is Cronus, a Titan who is a semi-primordial being from the second generation of gods after creation, and his mother is Philyra, a sea nymph—a beautiful creature that arose from the natural world as an expression of nature itself. His half-brothers include Zeus, Hades, and Poseidon.

Chiron has been depicted as having the appearance of a centaur, although he is not of the centaur race. He was abandoned at birth after his father had transformed into a beast to conceive him, and because he was the result of a rape, he was subsequently abandoned by his mother and exiled for his beastly form. His nephew Apollo found him and adopted him, nurturing his best qualities of intellect and creativity, teaching him the greatest of all knowledge, encouraging him to see past his own origin story and superficial semblance. Chiron was also a bearer of the raw spirit of prophecy and showed great aptitude for guidance and foreknowledge. He went on to became a respected mentor and coach for many of the greatest heroes of the pantheon including Jason, Perseus, and Heracles.

Zeus is said to have made Chiron a permanent feature of the night sky as a sign of respect to him for accepting death and trading his immortality for the freedom of Prometheus. He had defied the gods by sharing the knowledge of fire with mankind and was resigned to eternal torture. Centaurus is a constellation in the southern hemisphere consisting of twelve named stars with Alpha Centauri being the closest star system to Earth. This system is a binary system where two stars. orbit each other. A third star, Proxima Centauri, is a red dwarf and orbits the binary system on a much wider and elongated orbital path. This triple star system is the third brightest "star" in the night sky as it appears as a single point of light to the naked eye. The Omega Centauri globular cluster is part of this constellation and may contain up to ten million stars. This same location in the heavens is also associated with the Zodiac sign Sagittarius as the configuration is thought to resemble a half-human-half-horse which is drawing a bow and arrow.

The number of the beast, as described in the Bible, is something that probably scares most of us. It has come to be associated with war, tyranny, apocalypse, the antichrist, and even the end of humanity. I have worried so much about not only being him and having the gift, which is a battle in itself, but also bearing that supposed satanic number. I felt such despair and dread, terror and failure in facing these omens and understanding these signs. Nostradamus was the one to comfort me. He identified "Chyren" as a positive force who could do many great things. When I realised that the beast had many different sides, aspects, and forms, I found that it was something broad and symbolic, connecting the future to the past, history to prophecy, mythology to religion, science to pantheon, and a demonic power a saintly human nature.

I have thought quite a lot about what it means to be associated with the Chiron, and I do think that his peaceful nature, artistic talent, and vast knowledge are more symbolic than his external guise. In some depictions, he is fully human from the front, with a horse's body, hind legs, and tail extending from his lower back. In my mind, if this beast truly does represent me or Jesus in his new form, his horse's body merely represents his connection to the past, like his previous forms meandering across the map and looping throughout the past like a serpent's tail, with many threads of the past converging around him in the present, and symbolising his ability to connect us to the future—like so many of the past generations who still influence our world today. There is also the duality of his two opposing components: the primordial beast and beautiful nymph, like the joining of elements from the cosmic forces which made us, along with nature itself. He represents us humans and also something more, something that we cannot see or define. I also think he is emblematic of our animal origins and baser instincts but emphasises a spirit of peace that is connected to prophecy and knowledge.

It is really quite calming for me to relate to him, and it feels rather symbolic of my internal perspective on what the messianic prophet is. I am a freak in many ways. You would never know just by looking at me but I am part of the most unusual and rare, yet consistent supernatural recurrence in human existence. When people learn what I am they will all take notice. I may as well have horns and a tail for how different I am compared to everyone else that surrounds me. Even the source of this gift seems to be demonic and frightening, devastatingly powerful, and singular in it's existence. It is something so beastly and monstrous that it may just have the power blow open and snap shut the whole universe as if it were a piece of bubble gum.

Now that I have absorbed his story and gained some perspective on it, I felt calm, peaceful and more willing to bear that number. But I also think that some people may want to be part of the evil beast which conquers the world and subjugates the world's people. Some may even want to be the antichrist who fools or forces the world into worshipping him and his clan or their systems of power and wealth. There are other ideas that have been expressed about those times that warn us of temples, thrones, and crowns. It all seems so very shallow and hollow, so it's hard to imagine modern humans becoming so deliberately misled and detached from our shared reality.

One of my worst fears about these possible events is that these violent and egotistical people will treat him like a beast, re-enacting the stories of Isaac, Daniel, and Jesus all at once: imprisonment, torture, ritual sacrifice, and execution. Re-establishing a Dark Age empire of human sacrifice, superstitious belief, along with fabricated gods and idolatrous religion, combined with the worship of a class, race, bloodline, or a group of priests and king.

I am not a believer in the ritual sacrifice of any form of life for any purpose. I do understand that some traditions are communal feasts, and that is different. But to kill for the sake of killing, or as a demonstration of power, or because of superstitious belief, or as some kind of blood ritual, is purely primitive and insane, in my opinion.

Zarathustra

Zarathustra was an ancient Iranian prophet and the father of Zoroastrianism, a religion that still has believers today. He is said to descend from a line of prophets that originated in early Persia, and his teachings are thought to have helped inspire all of the Abrahamic religions and their texts. His holy book of religious text was called the "Avesta" and he spoke of three messianic figures called Saoshyant followed by an eventual saviour or righteous restorer called Shah Bahram.

His teachings appear to predate widespread writing, and his many followers had learned to recite his verses before they were written down generations later. It became the state religion of many Persian empires for over a thousand years. The style of his ideas is similar to, and compatible with, Hindu and other ancient religions that assigned the roles of nature's forces to their many deities. It can be difficult to understand if you don't speak the language, but it does appear to me that some of these gods were playing roles that were substituted for scientific explanations of the environmental forces experienced on Earth. These types of pantheons had supreme deities which were complemented by many other gods or forms that were mere expressions of the same supreme force that governed everything.

Zarathustra was heavily influenced by many of the very early religious ideas so his texts are in many ways compatible with the ancient mythologies along with the more modern Uni-god religions. Zoroastrianism has followers scattered across the map with it's largest following in India.

The Hindu religion is actually quite fascinating; I don't know as much about it as I might like to, but just as Zarathustra seems to have been describing some of the earthly forces of nature in his bible, Hinduism appears to describe the nature of the universe, the ethereal or spiritual realms, and even elements of theoretical physics—long before we had comprehensive scientific explanations or any type of visual interpretation of things like space time, gravity, creation, and evolution.

In the ancient world, religion was science, and throughout almost all religious cultures is an attempt to explain everything from the Earth's formation, the infancy of the universe, and even things like death, reincarnation, and a far-off future where humans would be powerful, knowledgeable, and possess the gifts of the gods—instant communication, flying through the sky, underwater travel, space exploration, and peering through portals to view live events unfolding on the other side of the world. These ideas are most obvious and evident in the Greek pantheon with figures such as Hermes (winged sandals), Poseidon (god of the sea), Ouranos (god of the sky and outer space), along with Helios, Horus, and the Norse deity Heimdall, who could all see across great distances.

Narasimha

Narasimha was the fourth Vishnu avatar of the Hindu pantheon. He intervened to protect a loyal believer who was also the son of a tyrant. He is known as the man-lion because of the form he took to break a curse and defeat the despot king. The king despised Vishnu and his honest followers as he wished to be worshipped as the primary deity and central god figurehead. The man-lion avatar is similar to Chiron in many ways but also like his primordial father Cronos because he could change form at will. Narasimha also defeated a dragon-like beast, comparable to the powerful demon-monster in Revelations or the serpent that Apollo defeated after his mother took refuge to give birth to him and his twin sister, Artemis/Diana.

Parashurama

The sixth Vishnu avatar in the Hindu religion was Parashurama. I think that his story echoes that of Osiris, Horus, and even Moses/Jesus. In one version of the myth he built an empire only to be killed by his brother, who stole the realm and became the king, subsequently installing an elite dynastic class of violent tyrants and dishonest generals. Parashurama was then reincarnated and had to rise back to power to kill his uncle and scatter the powerful and corrupt bloodlines that he had empowered. He had no choice but to take back the Kingdom and free the people from corruption and tyranny. It is a tale that is unmistakably similar to the story of Horus and his uncle Seth, who had killed his father, married his mother, and became a slaver and despot who forced the kingdom to worship him as the primary deity and divinely chosen god-king.

The coming task of Kalki, who is the tenth Vishnu avatar, will be to end the Kali Yuga (Age of Destruction), and usher in a new era of peace and prosperity. He is said to express his interpretation of the ambiguity of the pantheon and tell the tale of his belief in the supreme deity and how many forms can become one. Parashurama is also expected to appear alongside Kalki as a mentor and guide in the fulfillment of ancient prophecy in a futuristic world, similar to the Mahdi and Jesus.

The Kalki name is also derived from the word kal, meaning time, and it is claimed that he will be carried on a white horse. He will be accompanied by a parrot called Shuka, who represents the "all-knowing" (past, present, and future). Kalki also appears in some Buddhist and Sikh texts. Kalkin in Buddhism means righteous king or chieftain, and in Sikhism, he is described as the 24th avatar.

Hercules

Elements of the Parashurama story have been mirrored in many stories throughout the ages—not only with Moses but maybe also in the story of Jesus, who is predicted to return as a King to conquer Rome and Jerusalem and begin a golden age for humanity. I also see threads of the Jesus prophecy in the legend of Hercules, who was challenged to twelve labours by the gods and sabotaged by his wicked stepmother. He is said to have passed many trials and tests, defeating many ancient mythological creatures, including a sometimes "seven-headed beast."

Hercules was the centre of many cults of worship all around the Mediterranean, and these shrines and temples even made their way into Egypt after the campaign of Alexander the Great. German clans sang of him before battle, and some medieval French kings even claimed descent from him. Numerous Roman emperors claimed to be the reincarnated Hercules, and many royal clans of ancient Greece identified as "Herculeidae" and asserted their divine right to rule through their Herculean blood.

The Epic of Gilgamesh

Gilgamesh was a folk hero whose story is similar to that of Hercules and his saga probably inspired some biblical texts along with significant elements in the story of Noah. He is said to have to have travelled far and wide as he contended with various gods who tried to end him, killing monstrous beasts and creatures of mythology. The story originates in Sumer but seems to have been first recorded in early Babylon. He explored the ancient lands after a series of floods and quested to discover the whereabouts of a man called Utnapishtim who had built a boat to save his family and animals many generations before. Much like Enoch, Utnapishtim was granted immortality for his faith in the gods and became their messenger for his ability to persevere and survive the flood sent by them to wipe clean the noisy human cities that covered the earth.

The travels of Gilgamesh is believed to be the oldest recorded story in world history giving him the rare status of being older than the bible.

The Buddha

I deeply connected with Buddha's description of a spiritual being trapped in a cycle of earthly reincarnation. Plagued by suffering (dukkha) he desperately searched for an escape to heaven or a method of finding peace with his human immortality. I read the Dhammapada, and it does express the qualities of good-natured people. It describes how to avoid confrontation or find tranquility when dealing with negative people and stressful events. It teaches that hurtful people will ultimately only hurt themselves, and when you exhibit peace and harmony, it can only come back to you, multiplied. The book has many wise sayings and can help to focus a frustrated mind and encourage calm when dealing with difficult emotions that have exterior triggers.

He was born into nobility and chose to give up his status and wealth to wander the land searching for spiritual enlightenment and inner peace. He was born in Nepal but travelled extensively throughout India, Pakistan, and Bangladesh, teaching meditation and abstinence while taking a vow of poverty. He built up a monastic following, and the religion spread as far as China, Mongolia, Taiwan, and Japan. Buddhism is not based around a central deity or supreme god—it is a spiritual religion which suggests a belief that we are primarily ghostly entities and are only temporarily human. Its main focus is the human experience of discontent, discomfort, and disappointment. I think this flaw in our human nature is possibly due to our animal origins, how we are wired, and our evolution being dependent on our hunter-gatherer nature. Millions of years of gathering stock and foraging for supplies has translated in modern times into egotistically competing with each other for ownership of resources, and our obsession with amassing wealth and worldly belongings.

Although the Buddha is said to have achieved nirvana and escaped the earthly realm to reside in heaven, he has promised the return of another Buddha in the form of Maitreya, which means friendly and kind. This new Buddha has been described as a "world teacher of humankind," and in some texts, he is suggested to be a king in the land which is also the birthplace of Kalki. He is meant to be benevolent, gentle, and beneficial to all living things. It is thought that he will be the fifth Buddha and has a similar function to Kalki and Jesus. He is meant to lead humanity from the age of decline into an age of enlightenment, restore ancient texts, and is associated with time and immortality, along with love, wisdom, and the rediscovery of valuable ancient knowledge.

KHALIL KALIFA

I had originally chosen my pseudonym as a Hebrew name which I felt told my story and signified the sense of duality that I struggled with. Enoch Samyaza seemed fitting in a great many ways. The source material describes Enoch's angelic encounters and the visions of knowledge they shared with him such as electricity, global weather patterns, and even rare cosmic phenomena which sound like an accurate depiction of a neutron star. The book is attributed to Enoch but it clearly was not directly inspired or authored by the grandfather of Noah. I do think the story does represent the reincarnated prophet and I am sure it was inspired by the gift of prophecy and it's hosts.

I also think that elements of the story hint at man's destructive and greedy nature as well as the curse of being a lone prophet in crowd of power-seeking humans who desire to be kings with unadulterated authority. God may have rescued Enoch or even allowed me to visit the heavens but ultimately if the world becomes corrupt with widespread violence and networked criminality, there is no permanent escape or cleansing the Earth of barbarism. I/he can only aspire to repair the system or suffer the consequences. Eternally.

I have always liked the name Khalil. Even though the only Arab blood I have is probably very dilute and quite ancient, I still feel some loyalty to its origins and the fascinating stories and history surrounding its native lands. The Jews have only been around for a few thousand years and likely came from the mixed blood of Mediterranean and Levantine peoples. I find the idea of this mixed identity so interesting and fascinating that it has completely captured my mind's eye.

My experience of Heaven seemed to have been almost specifically Greek: a Greek human-like angel or deity, a white and blonde Angel Queen, marble pillars, and an ancient book of knowledge and prophecy that we are only now beginning to understand. The Greek pantheon is extremely extensive, well thought out, and accounts for almost every human tendency, possible skill or invention, and the many "godly" forces that govern the heavens and the earth. Their pantheon describes three generations of evolutionary creation that began with primordial gods, who were overthrown by their offspring, resulting in the Titans (like Kronos—time) and finally the more humanoid Olympians that we all know today (Zeus, Hades). It is mind-boggling to discover my genetic connection to the origins of these stories and the peoples they are associated with , and it is even more fascinating and unbelievable to think that I once stood next to what seemed like the very real inspiration for a story that could never be true.

The modern birthplace of civilisation, empire, organised religion, government, and messianism is the Levant. It is quite the original story and a strangely mysterious place and time to be connected to by blood—and even more so, spiritually. The greatest proofs of our ancient human society lay in these lands. Ingenuity, unity, collective belief, and obscure motivation still inspire and mystify us thousands of years later.

I had always assumed that I was 100% native Irish, but now I have come to understand something very different from what I was so very sure of. The more I investigate my experiences and the connections they suggest, the more I see a deeply cross-cultural narrative and a story of human unity and interconnectedness.

Al Khalil is a town in Palestine, and it is my understanding that in Arabic the word means friend. Khalifa means deputy or successor and is generally associated with Prophet Muhammad (PBUH) and the seat of power that was vacated when he died, triggering various power struggles and assassinations that continued for many generations, adversely affecting Muhammad's own descendants most of all.

I cannot say that I know a lot about Islam, nor Islamic culture, but I do feel a certain loyalty toward Muhammad, his people, and the Islamic religion.

He taught us a lot about "him," and it is comforting to know that I am not alone in my experience of angels. I have read that both Nostradamus and Joan of Arc had similar supernatural experiences, but Muhammad and his scribes made the belief in angelic super-beings a core tenet of the Muslim faith. That has made my experience feel much more like a privilege than a solitary struggle with reality. Without such detailed accounts of those unusual and unexpected events, such an incident would seem so improbable and unique that I would be forced to question my own psychological health and acuteness.

In a lot of ways, I can sense the presence of Muhammad, and I kind of feel like I know him, or that we might agree on many normally divisive or misunderstood subjects. I do feel like he knows my life and my mind, and it is reassuring to believe that he has accepted me as part of the prophetic line, as flawed and unknowledgeable as I might think myself to be.

I am not sure how I feel about what I am supposed to be. It is difficult idea to accept and even harder to understand. I cannot imagine that most traditional believers would accept me as any type of Messiah, Mahdi, avatar, or prophet. I do suspect that my existence as one of "him" will expose the obvious truth: that in many ways he is just an average human being, merely carrying a very godly and collectively human gift. No human being could be purely holy and infinitely wise without effort or aspiration, or of divinely flawless character. I am a weak and tiny human, but aren't we all in the presence of God?

I chose my pen name because it means friend or ally to the true caliph, Prophet Muhammad (PBUH). That part of me though, that is also part of "him," really does feel like an alter ego or a periodical but temporary persona. It may just be something that I must learn to be as opposed to something that I just am. This is why I actually think that a pseudonym is rather appropriate in many ways and for many reasons.

I do so very much want to be a friend to Palestine; they really do need their prophet, much more than Israel wants a messiah to be returned. And I also believe that Israel would only be too happy to wait for a Messiah if it meant more land and more time to pass the point of no return in its campaign of exceptionalism and privilege. And more living in a time warp where two thousand years of world history has disappeared, so they can stake their claim as the only true Hebrews and Abraham's only heirs. This idea of recreating a long-gone empire, with its temple, throne, and overpowered clergy, is a frightening concept to me. They are trying to revisit a time that has long passed, with the goal of becoming as powerful as the ancient and unbalanced empires of Egypt, Rome, and Babylon, the new empire that no one can defend themselves against and has special status under God.

But I also feel a strong obligation to the Jews. Though to be honest, I feel that loyalty more toward the victims of the Holocaust and the Nakba. I want to share in the struggle of identity with the "leftists" who resist the forced transformation and cultural conversion of Judaism and argue against the Zionist demands for loyalty to their radical ideology. I feel as though Israelis need to be saved from themselves and their manufactured reality, just as much as "traditional" Jews might want to be saved from Zionism itself.

I think that maybe Jesus and Daniel wanted to be saved from ancient Israel and it's royal clergy too, but with the new empire wanting to claim him as their throne and sought-after hive mind, there really was nowhere else to go. It was probably better to suffer and expose the true nature of the immortal imperial beast than to run and hide and possibly disappear forever. If he evanesced for too long, the story would be much harder for him to piece together or be obvious enough for everyone else to understand it.

The problem with vanishing is that when you find out what you are and how it works, you really want to reach your future self and tell them all the things that you wish you had known sooner. But the only way to do that is to pass the information along through everybody else, and in so many ways that is frustrating and often futile. Yet it can also be beautiful and harmonious. That means he also has to educate an entire generation just to re-educate his soon-to-be reincarnated self, possibly changing the psyche of world society forever. That really does sound like some type of spiritual or intellectual evolution, and for the whole colony, just like how basic cells and organisms communicate, sharing information throughout the entire group, even trading genetic information horizontally, without needing to reproduce a more diverse and intuitive offspring. I believe information can change us, and not just psychologically or spiritually but physically, and that can change us genetically. For him to grow, we must all grow with him!

Al Mahdi

The Mahdi is figure in Islamic prophecy who is said to appear alongside Jesus on his return to society. For a long time I did not really understand his role or importance in the story of Jesus. There are conflicting accounts of Muhammad's description of Al Mahdi among the four accepted Hadith (collections of sayings by The Prophet which were recorded by some of his closest companions). The most well-known and widely accepted narration speaks of him having an Arab complexion with long black curly hair, and a second suggests that he is white with a red complexion, similar to the baby Noah in The Book Of Enoch. Both versions say he has a red mole on his right cheek.

Previously, I was only familiar with the first but certain details did stand out to me. He is almost described in the same way that I might recount how Apollo appeared to me. This makes me wonder if when Muhammad (PBUH) was visited by Jibreel (Gabriel) did he see a man with brown skin and black hair. I am sure that these visions of angels are uniquely specific to the person that beholds them, and if another were to meet with the same entity, they would surely be more similar or familiar in appearance to that particular witness.

For quite a long time I wondered about the Mahdi and even believed that I needed to wait to speak of my ideas, or that I needed an ally to announce myself to the world. I thought he must be a sign of when the timing might be right for me to "appear." But a couple of months ago the situation changed in West Asia and I re-examined those particular hadith. I then discovered the second narrative on the Mahdi and began to realise that Al Mahdi is Muhammad and so maybe I could be him too.

I did not always have a red mole or scar on my face. Something was deliberately done to damage my skin around 2020, during the pandemic. I had a skin infection that was hard to cure and medications, cleansers, and creams all left my skin prone to sun damage. I was spending most of my time outside and did not realise that my skin barrier was permanently weakened. Personally if these hadith are about me I do not think that something like that should have been written down as it may encourage the mistreatment of someone. But there is also the possibility that those petty acts would have been committed against me anyway.

The Mahdi has many titles in Islam and was clearly highly respected by the Prophet and the companions. Muhammad (PBUH) is said to have directed that Al Mahdi would be part of "Ahlul Bayt" meaning he is part of Muhammad's closest family. Muhammad (PBUH), his cousin Ali, his daughter Fatima, and his grandsons Hasan and Husayn are the five members of this Holy House. Ali and both his sons were the first three of the Twelve Imams who are all martyrs and revered as saints in Shia Islam.

The Mahdi is referred to in numerous titles such as The Truth, The Guided One, The Awaited One, The Twelfth Imam, The Hidden Imam, The Remnant of God, and The Proof of God. He is also called something else which means "to rise alone." He is predicted to return to society alongside Jesus and will help to defeat tyranny, establishing peace and justice on Earth. He will also prepare us for the end times, spread the word of the Quran, redeem Islam, and confirm Muhammad as a true Prophet of God.

I may not be the prophesied Mahdi but if there is a chance for peace and stability for my distant relatives and his loyal believers – the peoples and places of "his" modern genesis - I want and need to deliver him back to them, and to all people.

The Divine Saviour

I am not trying to market myself as the saviour of the world or any type of divine being sent to us for purposes unknown, but I do believe in God's guidance and the many possibilities that come with such a misunderstood and fascinating ability. I do think that it can help and encourage us to transform and evolve into something better, something more than human. In some ways we already are something more with machines and modern technology, but this knowledge must be used wisely and fairly. It should be used to create a fairer and more balanced world, rather than a world which raises anyone above all others or abuses the knowledge that God has sent to us.

It is not up to him to save us; that is something we must do for ourselves. However, I do believe that this gift can aid us in our quest to live "forever" if we mirror the spiritual ideals that he has directly encountered and been embraced by. He does have access to a providence that belongs only to God, and there is a divine reason for something like that to exist at all.

Final Thoughts

I once thought that if I could summarise this entirely painful and recent chapter in this human story of mine and his in one sentence, it would be this:

The priesthood lusted after him, so they stole his blood, destroyed the temple, and lusted after him once more. This feels like the essence of my struggle and his curse—to be the one of a kind in a sea of unique similars. His mere existence invites power struggle and challenge and the rejection of the idea that any other person is better or more "worthy" of power and knowledge than ourselves.

This ghostly presence and ethereal consciousness is so much more than any single human mind or specific incarnation. We may never fully understand what he is, but we should be willing to allow him to move forward and accept change. He wants freedom, chance, choice, and new experience. We need interconnectedness and knowledge with fresh perspective, and an awareness of the sum of our collective behaviours. We need to integrate and allow him to travel from tribe to tribe, continually building something that becomes the newest piece in a great and ever-changing empire.

I sense that he has never really been allowed to make any decision for himself, as there are so many around him who would act threatened and excluded. I feel as though the various versions of this empire have stolen his bloodlines or wiped out his descendants. I fear that they are desperately trying to manipulate and control his many legacies—imprisoning and killing his avatars or absorbing, capturing, and exiling his descendants. Or ensuring that he is uneducated, poor, and without an honest audience.

Personally I think that he is a fluke and whatever it is that he has seems to be some kind of divine miracle. It is not a skill that the rest of us can learn or copy, so for that reason I am inclined to think that it is not a natural human ability. It must come from God or heaven or some related spiritual or cosmic ethereal force that we cannot measure or explain. It does seem to be a unique and necessary part of our reality. It is not like the type of genius that Einstein or da Vinci possessed. As rare as people with that calibre of talent or intellect are, he is something very different.

If one million human beings existed simultaneously he would only be one, and if eight or ten billion people existed at the same time he would still be just one. When he is not among us he has only just left and be will returned very soon. If his ability could be copied or mimicked or studied and learned it would have been done already. Or if his gift could have been stolen or confiscated and awarded to someone else it absolutely would have been done, many times over.

I do think that this anomaly is measurable and quantifiable, but that does not mean we can ever possess or fully control it. It can be captured, killed and even manipulated to certain degree but I believe he will always try to be independent, cautious, and intuitively obey the deep sense of purpose and balance that comes with using it. He can only be loyal to the logic and truth of the knowledge that he feels he has been consumed or created by. The things he sees, the places he can go, been taken to heaven to be shown belonging, purpose, and a love that is not transactional, these things can only change you for the better and I really do wish that we all could go there and understand it for ourselves.

It is a complex concept and beyond the understanding of normal human capacity, especially mine, but it is a gift of knowledge and so it can only be based on fact, freedom, and honesty. Acceptance is also a huge part of what it is because I or he did not consciously choose to be this, nor do we control the information and certainly not its source, it is something that we must try to understand together as one mind is clearly not sufficient to decipher such a strange cosmic force. This is how we were forged by the forces of creation and I cannot deny knowing this power to anyone. It is a part of us all but only one can be its custodian, guardian, and vehicle. It must surely pass along us all on its journey to possess its next host, and we should do our best by him, as he does for us.

I believe that he does possess (and maybe is) this uniquely human power, but its systematic appearance here on Earth definitely expresses some incomprehensible element of our universe and what it is that made us. This is why we should behave more like seekers and keepers of knowledge rather than gluttons for power and wealth. We are meant to share and cooperate not hoard or exclude. He may carry a unique ability that no two humans can ever simultaneously possess but every other person in the genepool has more freedom than he along with the potential to be better skilled or more talented at anything or everything else. I don't think that I am greater than anybody but I do think that we are all part of the same organism that may have been birthed up to 4 and a half billion years ago. I do believe that my loyalty should lie with benefiting that same organism—the colony of cells which we are all a part of, which may have been reproducing since our sun ignited, transferring heat and light to the primordial surface of our infant planet.

He may not always be visible, but he almost certainly is always among us. He might not feel like he is wanted or needed, but there surely are times when he must become involved in the affairs of the world. Sometimes we do need to collectively see the truth for ourselves, and society does regularly need a reset or an update as it drifts in the wrong direction because of geopolitics and the dishonesty of power retention. I do think that we need him but this gift can be hard to bear and it can be a lot of pressure and struggle to contain. It is a hugely overpowered ability that really should not be possessed by any man, and I wonder if any human mind is capable of bearing the stress and the weight of such enormous power when it seems to come from within, but its source exists very far outside of our known reality. He is not a god nor an angel, but merely a man who must resemble those ideals as best he can, in spirit and in mind, and avoid becoming a victim of his own ego, much like the "godkings" of old Egypt and Rome.

It is a battle, and a struggle like no other, and when he is not struggling against the great powers, he is fighting with his very own mind or the people that have tried to change it. But there does come acceptance and balance, but only after fear, delusion, and courage. I still feel like I am trying to earn whatever this is and I hope that I can use it for the good of us all. We should not be ambushing a child to cheat his spirit and break his mind. I think he should be old enough to possess a fully matured brain before using such a mighty and world-changing power. I think we humans are delicate and the mind certainly can snap, break, or fracture, but it can also heal and I pray that the world can too.

It is an incredibly perplexing and mystifying ability which has been stationed here on Earth as a permanent feature by an incomprehensible ethereal consciousness. It is a huge part of who we are but we will never fully understand the reasons why it has been given to us, it's mysterious source, or why and how it chooses its hosts. If it has been here since the beginning, it will certainly be with us until the end. And we must accept it as part of the nature of our existence.

There are many questions and few answers, but we are beginning to understand at least some of the elements involved in the story of creation and how life came to be. The universe is endless and ageless when we look at it though human eyes, but these are the days when we can understand that mechanical beast like never before. I sense that he feels a lost soul who has wandered the Earth since time immemorial but hopefully that means having enough time to gain insight, wisdom, and a matured spirit. With so many layers and many more perspectives to these stories, we can discover the questions and seek out the answers together. The answer might always be another question, but to understand the questions might just be the most comprehensive answer of all.

The End of the Beginning

THE NOSTRADAMUS PROPHECIES

CD XXXI (Century 4 Quatrain 31)

The Moon full in the night over the high mountain,

The new sage with a lone brain saw her,

By his disciples invited to be immortal,

Eyes to the south. Hands in bosoms, bodies in the fire.

CCC XXXV (Century 3 Quatrain 35)

From the very depths of the West of Europe,

A young child will be born to poor people,

He who by his tongue will seduce a great troop:

Rumour will grow in the kingdom of the east.

DC XVII (Century 6 Quatrain 27)

Within the Isles of five rivers to one,

Through the expansion of the great "Chyren Selin":

Through the drizzles in the air, the fury of one,

Six escaped, hidden in bundles of flax.

C L (Century 1 Quatrain 50)

From the three water signs will be born a man

Who will celebrate Thursday as his holiday?

His renowned, praise, rule and power will grow,

On land and sea, bringing trouble to the East.

CCC XCIV (Century 3 Quatrain 94)

For five hundred years more, one will keep count of him,

Who was the ornament of his time?

Then, at one stroke, great clarity will be given,

He who, for this century, will render them very satisfied.

DCCC XCIX (Century 8 Quatrain 99)

Through the power of the three temporal kings,

The sacred seat will be put in another place,

Where the substance of the body and the spirit,

Will be restored and received as the true seat.

C XCV (Century 1 Quatrain 95)

In front of a monastery will be found a twin infant,

From the illustrious and ancient line of a monk.

His fame, renown and power, through sects and speech,

Is such that they will say the living twin is deservedly chosen.

CC XXVIII (Century 2 Quatrain 28)

The penultimate of the surname of the Prophet,

Will take Diana for his day and rest:

He will wander far because of a frantic head.

And delivering a great people from subjection.

CM XXXIII (Century 9 Quatrain 33)

Hercules, King of Rome and of "Annemark,"

With the surname of the chief of triple Gaul,

Italy and the one of St. Mark to tremble,

First monarch renowned above all.

CX LXXII (Century 10 Quatrain 72)

The year 1999, seventh month,

From the sky will come a great King of Terror?

To bring back to life the great King of the Mongols,

Before and after Mars to reign by good luck.

CM XVII (Century 9 Quatrain 17)

The third one first does worse than Nero,

How much human blood to flow, valiant, be gone:

He will cause the furnace to be rebuilt,

Golden Age dead, new King great scandal.

DCCC LXX (Century 8 Quatrain 70)

He will enter, wicked, unpleasant, infamous,

Tyrannizing over Mesopotamia.

All friends made by the adulterous lady,

The land dreadful and black of aspect.

There will be a King who will give opposition,

The exiles raised over the realm:

The pure poor people to swim in blood,

And for a long time will he flourish under such a device.

www.ingramcontent.com/pod-product-compliance
Lightning Source LLC
Chambersburg PA
CBHW061101100726
47911CB00012B/342